SHATTERED

A NOVELLA ON LEGACY

T.A. GUILLORY

RIVER CITY SIREN PRESS

Copyright © 2025 by T.A. Guillory and River City Siren Press

All rights reserved.

No portion of this book may be reproduced in any form without written permission from the publisher or author, except as permitted by U.S. copyright law.

For my parents, who weren't perfect, but did their best.

PROLOGUE

His father's hands were much bigger than his own. Gordon held the wooden toy car steady in his hands as his dad, Dean, attached the small metal rod that held the front wheels on either side to the bottom of the block.

"Now these," Dean started as he held up two small magnets, "are going to give the car a bit more weight, which will help it speed up as it goes down the ramp. Where should we place them?"

Gordon nodded his head, focusing on the magnets. "Um... maybe here?" Gordon pointed at the front section of the car. "So that they help pull the car down faster?"

Dean raised his hand and stroked his walrus-like mustache. "Hmm. That's an idea. Are you sure that's where you want to put them?"

"Yeah... um... yeah!"

"Alright, you're the boss." Dean applied small dollops of glue to each magnet and stuck them to the front of the car. "Anything else you want to add?"

"No! It's ready! It's gonna win, Dad!"

"Damn right it is, boss!" Dean chuckled and tousled Gordon's hair.

Gordon stood up from the bench and made his way to his school entrance. Above the double doors hung a banner that read *Welcome to the First Grade Box Race! Start your engines!* Inside the halls were packed with Gordon's classmates and friends, each holding on to their own similarly shaped box cars. On the sides of the cars were different painted designs. Red cars with yellow lightning bolts. Blues with wave designs on the front and back. And each had their own unique additions such as nickels glued to the sides or small pieces of cardboard that looked like fins and wings.

The race was on as students were paired against each other. Two wooden ramps were set up in the school's large cafeteria. For each race, two students would stand behind the ramps and place their box cars at the top behind small barriers that kept them from rolling forward. At a countdown of *Three! Two! One!*, the barriers dropped simultaneously and the cars zoomed down the ramps, launching off the ends into a cushioned landing pad. Not all the cars made it to the end of the ramp. More than a few cars crashed early, flipping over as soon as they lurched forward; others veered right or left off the ramp, depending on where their weights were placed.

Gordon knew his car was going to be a winner. His dad helped him, and he knew everything. *He'll be so proud of me*, Gordon thought as he took his place, setting his white painted rocket ship car at the top of the ramp. Next to him, another student waved, a bright smile contrasting his dark skin as he set up a gray car with eyes and shark teeth on either side, a fin on top and at the end.

"Three! Two! One!," the announcer yelled, and the cars began their downhill plunge. Gordon's shark opponent seemed to sway from right to left, wheels nearly leaving the track. Gordon waited with baited breath for it to fall over the side. Then, with no warning, the end of Gordon's rocket lifted off the track and flipped, back over front, off the track and smashing onto the floor.

Gordon's throat tensed. Tears welled up in his eyes as he stared at the remains of his rocket on the tiled floor of the cafeteria. He felt his father's large hand on his shoulder, giving it a gentle squeeze before leaving his side to collect the broken pieces of the car.

Tears fell down Gordon's face on the car ride home. His father spoke to him from the front seat, but Gordon didn't understand what he was saying. All he could think was what a loser he was. *I'm useless. Dad hates me.* The tears and thoughts continued as they pulled into their driveway, while the pieces of his own car laid in a box in Gordon's lap.

"Come here, boss," said Dean, closing the car door behind him and walking to a small workbench that sat near the wall of the paneled house.

Gordon jumped down from the car and shuffled to his father. Dean reached down and took the box of Gordon's wreckage and set it on the bench. He then opened a cabinet and pulled out a small, dusty bronze trophy. The plaque read *Salesman of the Year, 1993*. He peeled off a large piece of beige tape and placed it over the plaque, then wrote with a large marker *Rocket Car Champion, 1996*.

Dusting it off with a rag, he handed it to Gordon. "I'm proud of you, Gordon. I know it didn't turn out like we wanted, but you tried. You built something that was yours and you put yourself out there. As long as you continue to try and be brave, you'll never lose."

Gordon's tears began to rain heavier than before. He launched himself into his father, trying to wrap his small arms around his father's large body. His father's massive arms held him close as Gordon cried into him.

"Now, what do you say we put this rocket car back together even better than last time, huh?"

Part One

Chapter One

The world was underwater, and Gordon had forgotten how to swim. The early morning sun crept through the windows. Gordon stood in his family's living room, the noises around him muffled. Jeanine, his mother, was on the phone, her voice panicked and rushed. "Yes, one-two-one-three West Napoleon. His name is Dean Guidry, he's my husband…" she continued as Gordon sank into the couch, his legs feeling like jelly. His father, Dean, sat in the nearby lazy boy struggling to put his shoes on.

He's struggling to use his hands all morning, lifting his arms and standing, the same issues from the night before when Gordon first recommended they call an ambulance in fear that his father was having a stroke. But they wanted to wait to see if the symptoms would pass for fear of looming medical bills. Next thing Gordon knew, the ambulance had arrived. The sirens sounded so far away. He couldn't focus on what the EMT's were saying to his parents. Now they had Dean on a stretcher and were wheeling him out of their house and into the flashing vehicle.

Minutes later Jeanine was driving to the hospital with Gordon in the passenger seat. Jeanine's hands were shaking as she guided the steering wheel. Gordon wondered if his hands would have been shaking to if he hadn't felt so numb. They drove in silence for what felt like hours, until they were parked and walking inside the ER of East Jefferson Hospital.

"We're here for Dean Guidry. I'm his wife, this is our son. He should have just been brought in," Jeanine said to the woman at the check in desk.

"Of course, ma'am. Just one second while I look him up." She looked at the computer in front of her then stood. "If you'll follow me."

Gordon and Jeanine walked swiftly behind the nurse through automatic double doors into a hallway lined with rooms filled with various doctors, nurses, and patients that led to a larger room, a nexus that led off into different hallways with a larger circular counter in the center full of men and women in blue, green and purple scrubs. The nurse gestured to a room and then hurried back to her check-in station. Inside the room, Gordon saw his father sitting in a paper-covered hospital bed, smiling and nodding to a man in a long white coat. He saw Gordon and Jeanine standing outside the room and nodded as if everything was fine.

Suddenly, as if hit with the blast of a shotgun, Dean fell back onto the bed. A series of beeps sounded from within the room and the doctor began to react quickly. Nurses from the center counter raced into the room, closing the door behind them. Jeanine let out a wail and began to crumble against Gordon as he caught her and did his best to stay strong and standing, his jaw set to keep himself from crying as well.

After a moment, a nurse asked them to follow her and led them to a room marked: "Family Grieving Room". It was about the size of a large closet, grey walls, two chairs and a table with a box of tissues, a dusty phone book and a landline phone. Jeanine dabbed her eyes with a tissue as she sat down. Gordon followed suit, leaning forward and clasping his hands together in front of him.

"We n-need to call y-your sister," Jeanine sputtered out.

Gordon reached into his pocket for his phone and found it empty. "I forgot my phone at home." Jeanine nodded and reached into her own pocket for her phone and handed it to her son. "Thanks." Gordon typed CHARLOTTE into the phone and his sister's information came up. And he started the call.

"H-hello? Mom? Why are you calling so early?" a drowsy Charlotte asked.

"Charlotte. It's Gordon. Um, Dad is in the hospital. We think he had a stroke; it's bad."

"What? You THINK he had a stroke! What did the doctor say?"

"They haven't told us anything yet. Wait, hold on Charlotte, I'll call you back in a minute." Gordon hung up his mother's phone as the door opened and a tall and slender clean shaven doctor in glasses stepped inside.

"Mrs. Guidry?" He nodded to Jeanine. "I'm Dr. Kirk-Patrick. I've been tending to Mr. Guidry. Your husband suffered a major stroke, and then a heart attack. We lost his heartbeat..." He paused for a moment and took a deep breath. Gordon wanted to scream at him to say something else. Anything to fill the gap of silence. "But we were able to get it back. We're sending him in for surgery now."

"Can we see him first?" begged Jeanine.

"I'm afraid not. They're already prepping him in the O.R. But we're setting up a room for him. Once it's ready a nurse will take you there to wait. But Mrs. Guidry, I need to impress upon you that even if the surgery goes well, Mr. Guidry's stroke was severe. We don't know the full extent of the damage yet, but it's very likely he's suffered permanent paralysis. He's going to need around-the-clock supervision and physical therapy. And adding the heart attack puts him in a very precarious situation. He may not have many years left after this event."

"H-how many, would you guess?"

"My best estimate? I would give him five years.

CHAPTER TWO

"Mr. Guidry, you were the first to discover the body, is that correct?" asked the short woman with a round face. One hand held a notepad, the other a pen, scribbling hastily. She looked up at Gordon from her notes, her eyes staring into his. "Mr. Guidry?"

"Hmm?" Gordon responded. *What body-? Oh.* "Uh, yeah. Yeah, I did."

"Can you tell me what time this was?"

"It was about, I don't know, four thirty-ish, I think?"

"Four-thirty?"

"Yeah. Yes." *Was it four-thirty? Maybe four-forty-five. Fuck, what time is it now?* Gordon swayed, shifting his weight from one foot to the other.

Five years after Dean Guidry's stroke, the Guidry family had fallen into a new normal routine as they cared for Dean in his paralyzed state.

"Can you tell me what you were doing before then? Where were you?"

"Um, yeah." *Too far. Slammed the door. Stormed out.* "Had to run an errand." *Had to get out of the house, had to think.*

"An errand?"

"Yeah, went to go get a smoothie." The officer shifted her mouth and began writing in the notepad once more. Gordon followed the back and forth motion of the pen.

"What happened when you got home?

"I walked inside, saw my dad sitting in his wheelchair; he usually sits there watching TV. I said *Hey*. He, uh, he didn't respond." Gordon felt a few drops of water land on his head and saw a few more landing on the officer in front of him. Clear drops of rain landed on the shiny, gold badge pinned to her chest, dripping down to a name tag that said "Bennett."

"Mr. Guidry?"

"Hmm? Yeah?"

"I'm sorry, I know this is hard, but I need you to focus right now, okay?"

"Yeah. Right." *You try fucking focusing.*

"What happened next?"

"I shook my dad a few times. Patted his face a bunch, yelled at him, tried to get him to respond. He didn't. His eyes were kind of rolled back, his cheeks were purple, his jaw just kind of hanging open."

"What was your father's name?"

"Dean Guidry."

"How old?"

Shit, uh, he was... "Sixty-three."

"Mr. Guidry, when I arrived he was lying on the floor, but you say you found him in his chair?" Her pen walked across her notepad.

"Yeah, he was in his chair. The paramedics put him on the ground when they got here."

"Your father was in a wheelchair, what medical problems did he have?"

How much time you got? "A few. Um, two heart attacks in the 90's, I guess around '97. Long time diabetes, runs in the family. Another major heart attack in 2008 and a massive stroke, left him paralyzed on the right side, couldn't speak that well after."

"I see. Please continue, Mr. Guidry."

Gordon sighed, raindrops falling onto the lenses of his glasses, blurring his vision. "I called 911. She, uh, the operator, I mean, she talked me through C.P.R." *Had to pump his chest fifteen, or, no — was it thirty times, then breathe?*

"Was there any response to the C.P.R.?"

"No." Gordon gazed past the woman and over to his sister, Charlotte. She sat on the green wooden swing hanging from the cypress tree that had always been there. Large round sunglasses were perched atop her auburn hair, her eyes staring at nothing as her fingers picked at faded green wood chips from the swing. He looked back to Officer Bennett, who was staring at him. "Uh, the operator wanted me to get him out of his chair, but he was too heavy."

"How long before the paramedics arrived?"

An eternity. "A few minutes? I'm not really sure; I was still doing C.P.R. when they got here. They took over and I stood back." *Out of the way. Let them do their job.*

"Mr. Guidry, was there anyone else in the house? Did someone come over?"

Charlotte. "Charlotte did."

"Your sister?"

"Yeah, she usually comes by in the evenings, helps me look after Dad." Bennett nodded, her eyes shifting back to her notepad. *Is she even writing anything or is she just doodling?* "She came in behind the paramedics, just stood there, staring at them, at Dad." *The look on her face was...* Gordon looked back to his sister. Her eyes were wide, her face still, just staring ahead of her. *Like that.* "I went to her, pulled her outside, told her pretty much what I'm telling you." *She started to cry. I hugged her, felt her shaking against me.*

"Where was your mother at this time?"

"On her way home from work, I guess."

"You guess?"

"I tried calling her after I told Charlotte what happened, but she never answered. I figured she probably forgot her phone at her office again." *Of all the times to forget that.* "She was late though, later than usual, but she'd mentioned picking up dinner on the way home."

"What's your mother's name?"

"Jeanine. Uh, Jeanine Guidry." Gordon's attention was once again drawn to Charlotte, who moved from the swing and towards their mother on the other side of the porch. Their mother was the same height as Charlotte, shorter than Gordon, with her reading glasses perched atop curly brown and gray hair. Her face had fallen, her cheeks wet. Charlotte was putting her arms around her, and they both began shaking as quiet sobs left them. Gordon let out a drawn-out sigh. Rain was falling on his head harder, bigger drops sliding down his face. His hand reached to touch his cheek, feeling the wet from his skin. *Just more summer rain.*

"Mr. Guidry?"

"What?" *Shit.* "Sorry. Yeah. Where were we?"

"Can you tell me what happened when your mother arrived?"

"I didn't notice the car pull up, just heard the door close. She ran up to the house. We followed her inside. The paramedics had set up this." Gordon gestured with his hands in an arch. "This thing, a machine, was pumping my dad's chest. They'd put an oxygen mask on his face. One of the paramedics, the woman–" Gordon nodded his head to a petite woman with blonde hair wrapped in a bun speaking to Charlotte and their mother. "—she told Mom they were giving him a fighting chance." *Bullshit.* "I guess, uh, it was ten minutes after that they, uh, turned off the machine and covered him with a sheet. Charlotte started crying again, my mom, uh," *Screamed? Sobbed? Yelled? I don't know how to describe it.* "She kneeled next to, uh, to the body."

Gordon took a long deep breath. Behind Officer Bennett, two men in black suits were rolling a stretcher out of the house, a black bag containing his father laid on top of it. Charlotte and their mother stood to the side, watching them roll him away. Charlotte's sunglasses now covered her eyes; she must have put them on at some point. *To hide her crying?*

"After that, I came out here to make some phone calls. Friends. Family. Mom and Dad's pastor. And..." Gordon looked at Officer Bennett once more, the notepad was gone, the pen barely sticking out of her front pocket next to her badge. "And then you and I began talking."

"I see. Mr. Guidry, is there anything else you can tell me? Some detail you might have overlooked? Was your father acting unusual when you last saw him?"

Too far. Too far. "No. He seemed like he always did. Just another day."

"Did he try to communicate something to you?"

Too far. "Just, 'too far.' Those were really the only words he could put together after his stroke."

"Do you have any guess as to what might have caused his death?"

Gordon scoffed, sliding his hands into his pockets, the fabric wet from rain. "Take your fucking pick!" He stopped, closed his eyes and took a breath. "Sorry. I don't know, I guess it could be any number of things. Probably another heart attack."

Bennett continued to stare at Gordon for a few moments before reaching into her back pocket and pulling out a small white card, holding it out to him. "I know this is a difficult time, Mr. Guidry. But, if you remember anything else, please call me." Gordon grabbed the card and looked at it. *Sarah Bennett.*

"Yeah. You got it."

Gordon stepped away from Bennett, walking under the dry cover of the porch, running his hands through his wet hair, shaking it out and slicking it back out of his face. He removed his glasses and wiped them with his shirt then slid them back on. Charlotte had made her way over to him, her round sunglasses still on her face, tear stains trailing beneath them. "You okay?"

Gordon looked to her eyes, or where her eyes would be behind the dark lenses, and saw his reflection. His eyes were still, his mouth still. No tear stains ran from his eyes, nor had his face fallen. "Yeah, I'm okay." *No, I'm not.*

"Ms. Guidry, can I speak with you for a moment?" Gordon hadn't realized the short officer had joined them.

Charlotte reached out and touched Gordon's shoulder, then stepped away with Bennett.

"Gordon?" His mother had stepped towards him. The mascara around her eyes was messed up, and her hand held a tissue just under her nose. "Did, uh, did your father try to say anything before you left?"

Gordon stared back at his mother, "Um."

'Too far.' Dad was in his wheelchair in the home office, I was in front of him.

'I don't know what that means,' I said, which must have been the thousandth time.

'Too far. Too, too far. Ooooh,' Dad shook his head, patting his chest with his left hand, the only one that worked.

'Okay. Okay, is something wrong? Do you need me to get something? Do you need me to do something?' Dad shook his head. He kept acting like he was reaching for something behind me. All that was behind me was a filing cabinet. We'd done this routine over and over, this guessing game of figuring out what he needed to say.

'You need to give me a clue, Dad. Something,' I pleaded.

'Too... Too far! Ugh! Too far! Too, too, TOO FAR!' he yelled, rubbing his face in frustration.

"I don't know what too far means! Are you uncomfortable?'

'Too far! Too far! TOO! FAR!' He grabbed my shirt, yanking me forward then pushing me back. 'Too far!'

'I don't know what you want me to do!' I had no idea I was yelling.. 'I don't know what you want me to do!'

"TOO FAR! UGH! Too far. Too far." Dean looked to Gordon, his brow furrowed, his hand on his chest.

'Fuck! I'll be back in a few minutes.' I walked out. I was frustrated. Angry. I got in my car and drove. I was only gone for-

"Gordon?" Jeanine had placed her hand on his shoulder. "Did he try to say or do anything?"

Gordon looked at the faded black mascara running down his mother's face. Her hand was shaking on his shoulder.

"No. No, nothing really." *Too far.*

Chapter Three

Three days after Dean Guidry died, Gordon sat at their family's dining room table: a dark, wooden surface that was once neatly set up for occasional shared meals. That day, it was covered in scattered papers, envelopes ranging from small letter envelopes to large manila folders, and greeting cards with words like "sorry" and "loss" written on the front. He stared at the papers in his hand, scanning the words over and over. Each time, the letters became an alphabet soup. Admitting defeat, he let the papers fall to the table, taking off his black rimmed glasses and rubbing his eyes.

Between reaching out to family and friends and organizing their finances, Gordon was exhausted. He picked up his phone to check the time: 8:34 p.m. Below the numbers were countless missed calls and text messages asking for details of his father's death, funeral arrangements, and questions about what casseroles to bring. He set it back down and stretched, running his fingers through his short brown hair and scratching his bearded chin. With a deep sigh, he picked up the discarded papers and tried reading them one more time.

The letter on top was from his parents' church, addressed to The Guidry Family. *Dear Jeanine, Gordon, and Charlotte...* The first paragraph offered condolences on Dean's passing, and the second shared fond memories of Dean and his time with the church. The third paragraph began to break down the funeral services the church offered, flower arrangements, the church choir, and the associated costs. Behind the letter was another bill for cremation costs. His eyes shifted from the pages in front of him to a large stack of papers to his right. *Medical bills*, he thought to himself.

Picking up a smaller envelope from the church. Gordon pulled out a greeting card. Small and rectangular, the greeting card had a simple cross on the front against a deep red background. He opened it and found a few more lines about how sorry they were to hear about Dean's passing and a small photograph. The smiling faces of his parents stared back at him, Dean and Jeanine, surrounded by children with varying degrees of brown and tan faces holding up a colorful banner thanking the church for their help. Gordon remembered when this photo was taken, how proud his parents were when they talked about the work they were doing after a heavy storm flooded some of the neighborhoods outside of New Orleans.

The front door opened and Charlotte stepped inside. Lynn followed closely, holding Charlotte's hand.

"Hey, little brother," Charlotte said quietly. She walked to Gordon and gave him a one armed hug. Gordon returned it and patted his sister's back and then hugged Lynn. "What is all this?"

"Bills." Gordon pointed to each stack of papers in turn. "Medical, condolences, and now, funeral. Some cards people have dropped off with some food. The rest is bills, receipts, stuff I'm trying to sort through to figure out what needs to be paid and when. Haven't had a chance to go through it all yet. Ma just stuffed all of this into the filing cabinet, no real organization, so... it's a lot." Gordon held up a letter in his hand, then set it down on the table. He looked at his sister; her usual large sunglasses sat atop her head, and a redness stretched under her eyes that nearly matched the dark red of her hair.

"Is that Charlotte?" a voice yelled from the other side of the house. Jeanine walked into the room, extending her arms towards her daughter.

"Hey, Ma," Charlotte said, hugging her mother.

"Hi, Sweetheart." Jeanine lingered in the hug, then looked at Lynn. "Oh, uh. Hi, Lynn." Jeanine started to go for a hug, but stopped, quickly switching to a handshake. "Good to see you."

"Hello, Mrs. Guidry," Lynn said, letting go of Jeanine's hand.

"Please, you know to call me Jeanine," she said politely, quickly looking from Lynn to Charlotte. "Both of you, sit, sit. Would anyone like some iced tea?"

"Yes, thank you," responded Lynn.

"None for me, Ma." said Charlotte, waving her hand.

Gordon merely shook his head. As Jeanine left for the kitchen, Gordon handed Charlotte the letter about the funeral and cremation costs. Charlotte scanned it, her eyes going wide as she showed it to Lynn.

"Seriously? It costs more to die than to get married!" Lynn said, handing the papers back to Charlotte, who let out a short laugh.

"I haven't asked Ma yet, but..." Charlotte leaned in towards Gordon. "Have they... have they figured out how Dad died?"

"Nothing official. After his stroke he had so many health problems, they said it could have been anything, but most likely a heart attack." Gordon cleared his throat. "They said it was probably quick..."

"Gordon, honey, could you give me a hand?" Jeanine called from the other room. Gordon got up and went to the kitchen. "Can you just take that to Lynn?" Jeanine said, gesturing to the iced tea on the counter, poured into a flimsy red plastic cup. "I'm warming up some food for everyone. Lord knows people have brought enough for us to share."

Gordon grabbed the cup of iced tea and stepped back toward the dining room, then stopped. Sitting at the table, Charlotte's head was buried in Lynn's shoulder, her body shaking, her arms holding Lynn tight. Lynn held Charlotte just as closely, stroking her hair as tears quietly streamed down her dark skin.

"I know, baby. It's going to be okay," Lynn said.

It was early afternoon the next day when a knock sounded on the door. As Gordon opened it, he saw a tall man with buzz cut gray hair and a big smile wearing a police uniform staring at him. "Hey, Gordon! I was lookin' for your mamma," Officer Steven Comeaux said, making an effort to look around Gordon's head into the house.

"Sorry, Uncle Steven. You just missed her. She went to the church to talk with them about the funeral." Gordon eyed their family friend up and down. His badge was pinned to his chest, with the words *New Orleans Police* engraved on it. On his neck, Gordon could see the corner of a fading tattoo sticking out of the shirt collar; a blue stripe with white stars, and red on both sides. Gordon had seen the full confederate flag tattoo before. Fishing trips with his dad, or barbecues where Steven was dressed more casually in t-shirts and jeans. As a kid, he didn't know what it meant. Now, he frowned at the sight of it.

"Oh, well, I just needed to holler at her 'bout something, I'll catch her later. Hm, would you mind if I came in for a moment?"

"Now's not really a good time," Gordon responded, gently beginning to close the door.

Steven's hand stopped the door, holding it open. "Just for a moment, please?"

Gordon sighed. "Sure." He stepped back, letting the tall cop inside.

Steven took a look around the room, letting out a deep sigh. "I'm sorry about Dean. He's a, um, I mean, he was a good man. A good friend." He took a step toward the dining room table, reaching out and moving some of the papers around. "Hell, when we were younger, we got up to all sortsa trouble!" He laughed as he began shuffling through the family bills, his hand moving from stack to stack. "I was hoping I could have something of his, just a keepsake." Steven's hand seemed to stop on a particularly large envelope.

"I'm sure Ma could give you something after the will is taken care of." Gordon stepped forward, leaning in front of Steven to move the stacks of his family's private information away from the nosy officer. Steven's hand gripped the envelope, pulling it suddenly, causing the stacks to fall from the table, scattering across the floor.

"Oh, now, I'm so sorry about that, son. Here, lemme' help with that."

"No! No, I got it." Gordon put his body between Steven and the mess. "I'm kind of in the middle of something here, but I'll have Ma give you a call. We can give you a keepsake once we've gone through the will and have everything settled."

Steven looked at Gordon, his eyes wide and nostrils flaring for just a moment before turning back into the smiling man Gordon knew so well. "You're right, of course. Just, out of sorts, missin' my friend." Steven began walking towards the door. "Well, just let your momma know I stopped by. Anything else I can do for you?"

"No, I think we're good, Steven."

The policeman nodded. "Alright then, Gordon. I'll see y'all at the funeral. And, again, I'm sorry about Dean. I'm gonna miss him."

Gordon closed and locked the door after Steven, watching through the window as the cop car pulled away. He sat back down at the table and resumed trying to organize the bills into their stacks and by their date. *What was he looking for?* He rearranged the papers back into their stacks one by one. Funeral. Medical. Monthly bills. Funeral. Medical.

Monthly- Gordon's hand grabbed a particularly large envelope. He thought he could feel cloth beneath the paper, and the hard bulges of a few solid objects. Turning it over in his hands, he recognized it as the envelope Steven had tried to grab that caused the piles to fall.

He slid his finger into the crack of the envelope to break the seal. Reaching inside, he took out a heavy, white cloth that was wrapped around a bulky silver ring, and a medallion bearing a red cross. He picked up the ring and turned it over in his palm, and his heart sank. On the old, silver band, he saw the design of the confederate flag. He dropped the cloth and its contents on the table and looked back into the envelope.

One after the other, Gordon pulled out black and white photos and what looked like an old newspaper clipping. *NEGRO FOUND DEAD.* Gordon's hands began shaking as he read through the news clipping and then looked through the photographs. Old black and white photos of white men and women with their hands raised in the air, some holding torches, others guns, some in white robes.

His eyes were wide, breathing heavily. His fingers loosened and the pictures tumbled to the table. One of them turned over, revealing the white back of the photo, words written across it. *Dean, Jeanine, Steven Jr., Steven Sr. The South will rise again!* Gordon turned over the picture and immediately threw it down. Staring back at him were the younger faces of his mother, his father, Steven, and a man in an old police uniform that looked similar to the man that just left his house, standing together in front of a burning cross. He began to shove them all back into the envelope, forcing his family's skeletons back into their closet. The last thing he put back was the white cloth, but he lurched back when he noticed two holes in the front of it. *Not a cloth. A mask.*

Gordon stood up. He began pacing back and forth, his head in his hands and heart pounding in his ears. The photo of his parents and their relief work were scarred by the ghostly image of his parents and the burning cross behind them. His pacing became longer and longer, from the dining room to the kitchen, then from the dining room to the hallway. He stopped suddenly and looked around him. The walls on both sides began to close in on him as he looked at pictures of his family. Vacations, school pictures, graduation photos. His and his sister's smiling faces seemed to turn to frowns.

His eyes locked onto one photo. Gordon must have been six or seven at the time, wearing a dark blue shirt and shorts. In his hands was a toy car he had made with his father, who sat next to him. The memory began to expand as he remembered the box car race he had entered.

His car didn't win that day. It barely made it down the ramp before it veered off onto the floor. His dad sounded disappointed, and then angry when another boy named Darnell won. On the ride back, he remembered his father talking about cheating, about how that boy shouldn't have been allowed to take part in the race. But, this photo is what he'd passed by in the hall over and over, this photo of him and his dad working on a toy car, a fond memory suddenly souring.

On the wall, the picture's frame was crooked. He looked down and saw pieces of glass, and heard it crunching under his feet. A few drops of red, then more. He looked down at his fist and saw a few small cuts and tiny shards of glass sticking in them.

Gordon stood in Charlotte's and Lynn's apartment around the counter that separated their kitchen and living room. the envelope lay between them.

"Fuck!" yelled Charlotte, breaking the silence.

She pushed away from the counter and moved through the kitchen. Opening one cabinet, she pulled out three glasses, then opened the refrigerator and pulled out a tall clear bottle half-filled with a pink liquid. She returned to the counter and filled each glass, passing them to Gordon and Lynn before pouring one for herself, finishing it quickly, and pouring a second.

Gordon accepted the glass with his left hand, while his right lay on the counter covered in bandages. Behind him on his sister's couch was a duffel bag full of his clothes, computer, phone charger, an overnight kit with toothpaste and a toothbrush: things he would need for the next few nights until he figured out where he would live. He had no desire to live in his mother's house. Not anymore.

He sighed and took his phone out of his pocket and saw the screen full of missed calls and text messages from his mother.

> Mom: Y r papers on the floor? How did this picture break?

> Mom: Gordon?

> Mom: Where r u? R u alright?

Gordon clumsily tapped a message with his left thumb.

> Gordon: Fine. At Charlotte's. See you at funeral

He reached for the news clipping, then began typing on his phone.

"What are you doing?" Charlotte stared at her brother.

"Getting the facts."

"Gordon..." Charlotte's voice was shaky.

"January 3rd, body of negro male David Harris found. Lieutenant Steven Comeaux of New Orleans Police Department says killers will be found and prosecuted. So he was covering them up?" asked Gordon, picking up the clippings and reading through them again.

"Gordon, stop!"

Gordon turned towards his sister. Next to her, Lynn's face was in her hands, her body shaking. Charlotte reached for Lynn's shoulder, but Lynn shrugged her off. She stood and walked to their bedroom, closing the door behind her.

"What do I do, Charlotte?" Gordon asked, searching for the answer in her face. She remained quiet. "Dad's funeral. I'll show the photos at dad's funeral. Step up to the microphone and show everyone who our parents really are."

"Gordon, no," pleaded Charlotte. "This is horrible, but—"

"But what? Our parents kept this secret from us, from everyone, and now we give them a pass? No. I... I need to do something. I'll do it at the funeral."

Later that night, Gordon laid on his sister's couch, staring up at the white popcorn ceiling. What was he going to say? He was about to shatter the reputation his parents had built, pull out the skeletons he so desperately wanted to hide earlier, and put them on display.. And what was he going to say?

Outside he heard the clickity-clack of the street car, growing louder as it approached, then softer as it sped away down the avenue. Through the apartment's thin walls he could hear Charlotte and Lynn's muffled voices, their hushed sobs. He loved Lynn like another sister for the three years he'd known her. She made Charlotte happy. But his parents always struggled to accept her. Now, he wondered if it had more to do with the color of Lynn's skin than Charlotte's sexuality. He remembered just last night, something so subtle, but so loud: the flimsy plastic cup instead of the glass set his mother always used for guests.

Gordon and Charlotte sat in the front pew of their parents' church. Lynn was noticeably absent from Charlotte's side. Around them, members of the church spoke quietly and shared their untainted memories of Dean Guidry. Easels sat against the walls with blown up pictures of Dean and Jeanine. Next to the photo of their relief efforts, Gordon saw a photo of his dad standing behind a table wearing an apron and handing a box of food to an older black woman. *Did he genuinely care? Or was this all a show?*

Jeanine approached them, her eyes going wide at the bandages on Gordon's hand. "Gordon, what happened, sweetie?"

"It's fine, Ma," Gordon responded.

"Just tell me what happened? Did you cut it on the frame's glass yesterday? What happened Gordon?" Jeanine fussed with Gordon's hand as she sat next to them. Charlotte, her eyes covered by her sunglasses, tears falling beneath them, abruptly stood up and moved to the back of the church.

"Charlotte's upset. I'm going to go sit with her. I'll, uh, see you after the service, Ma," said Gordon, pulling his bandaged hand away from her and standing up. Jeanine leaned back, furrowing her brow as she watched Gordon walk away.

From the last row, Gordon watched as the pews in front of them filled with friends of his parents. Some he recognized, others he'd never seen before in his life. In the front pew, he could see his mother, noticeably crying, speaking to Steven, who was dressed in a formal police uniform. As they spoke, he saw them stealing glances at him and Charlotte in the back row. Gordon sighed, pulling the envelope out of his suit jacket pocket. He stared at it, turning it over in his hands, running his fingers over the edges.

Throughout the service, friends of Dean Guidry stepped up to the podium and told the stories they remembered most about Gordon and Charlotte's father.

"I remember one time..."

"You should have seen Dean..."

"When you met Dean, you met a friend..."

Finally, it was Gordon's turn to speak. As he stood up, he felt Charlotte grab his hand. He looked at his sister. Tears slowly ran down her cheeks as she shook her head.

He squeezed her hand, then let go. He walked slowly down the aisle, the eyes of everyone on him. Some looked at him, then to Charlotte and his mother. Confused looks painted their faces. After what seemed an eternity, Gordon reached the podium. He gazed out at the crowd before him, his eyes landing on his mother. She was crying and wiping away her tears with a white handkerchief.

Gordon once again pulled out the envelope from his pocket and stared at it. He took a deep breath, then looked out at the congregation. Behind his mother, he met Steven's gaze. He watched as recognition changed his face from mourning to anger. "Dean Guidry... My father..." The words were hard to say. The black and white photos were fresh in his memory, but so was the picture of him and his father and his race car, the image full of color. He focused on that image, in its frame on the wall. A lump formed in his throat. He tried to clear it. Gordon looked back at the crowd, at his crying mother, his sister. "My... My father was..." Before him were the faces of the people who knew his parents enough to mourn his father's death. Many wiped tears from their eyes but still held smiles from the fond stories before. He looked at the envelope one last time, then slid it back into his pocket.

"My father wasn't perfect. But he was my father. I remember when I was young, six or seven maybe. He helped me build this little toy car for a race. They gave us the pieces we needed to put it all together, the wooden shape of the car, the wheels, and the weights to help it move down the track. He..." '*That boy shouldn't have been able to take part in the race!*' his father's voice echoed in his head. "He helped me put it together, helped me paint it. But, when it came to putting the weights on the car, he said he wanted *me* to put them where I thought they should go. So I put them all on the front of the car, thinking that when it went down the ramp, it would gain speed. And it did, so much speed, it veered off the track and onto the ground." The crowd laughed, Gordon's lips formed a soft smile. "But he was proud of me, that I made my own mistakes and learned from them. I think... I think he wanted me to grow into a better man than he was, because he wasn't perfect."

"You said such nice things about your father..."

"I sure am gonna miss him..."

"If there's anything you need, just call us..."

The service ended. Their father's friends stopped to say goodbye to Gordon and Charlotte before moving onto the reception. As the last mourners stepped out of the church, Steven and Jeanine approached them. Steven placed his hand on Gordon's shoulder. "Listen, son, I know you think you know what you found, but... well, it was a long time ago. I'm gonna need that envelope."

"Please Gordon. I know it's difficult for you to understand. You should have never found that. It was a long time ago. Things were... different," said Jeanine, quietly.

Gordon looked at the police officer. His coat had pins and badges representing his service, but he knew that flag was lurking behind his uniform. "Whatever these pictures say, they're going to say it to the public. Whatever you did or didn't do, will be found out. I'm going to make these public."

"Gordon, no! Please, don't do this," cried Jeanine, reaching for her son's hand.

"No, Ma. Dad's funeral wasn't the place to shatter others' ideas about who he was." Gordon stopped and clenched his jaw as his hands began to shake. "But this will be made public. I'm not going to protect you or Dad because of who I *thought* you were."

"Now listen here, boy," Steven shouted, leaning closer to Gordon.

In a flash, Charlotte was standing between Steven and her little brother, her hand moving faster than Gordon could see. A large red mark was blooming on Steven's face as he stepped back, shocked. "You try to touch my brother again, and I will fucking kill you."

Steven looked at Charlotte, his eyes and nostrils wide, fuming. "Is that a threat, little girl?"

"It's a goddamn promise."

PART TWO

Chapter Four

D usk was falling. Beneath the amber sky, cicadas buzzed in the trees in front of the apartment. Gordon and Charlotte sat in plastic folding chairs on the small, second story balcony, two cans of beer between them on a green plastic table. Gordon had taken off the suit jacket and loosened the tie from the funeral. Charlotte still wore her black dress but had added bright pink pajama bottoms to the ensemble and sat cross legged in the chair.

Gordon reached into his pocket and pulled out a long vape pen and took a drag. A small blue light cast subtle shadows on his face, accentuating the bags forming under his eyes and his sunken cheeks. Without a word, Charlotte held her hand out to Gordon, opening and closing her hand. He watched her, then looked at the vape as he let the vapor drift lazily from his lips.

"Thought you were quitting?"

"I'm no fucking quitter."

Gordon handed her the vape pen and watched as she took her own long drag. The blue light reflected in her sunglasses, still covering her eyes despite the growing dark. Tear streaks still stained her cheeks. For the first time, Gordon noticed how gaunt his sister's face had become over the past week.

"Um, how was the funeral...?"

Gordon turned to see the sliding door to the apartment open with Lynn standing just inside.

"It was... well, it was." Gordon stood and offered his seat to Lynn, but she shook her head, then focused on picking at the chipped paint of the door frame.

"Did you... you know?"

"No," Charlotte cut in, still staring ahead at the setting skyline. "And all the skeletons are still uncomfortably in the closet."

"Oh... I think that's for the best," replied Lynn, before shutting the door and retreating further into the darkened apartment.

Charlotte let out a quick sob, tears streaming down her face again. Gordon opened and then closed his mouth. He reached over and placed his hand on his sister's shoulder, feeling her shake with each quiet sob.

Lynn sat in the bedroom she shared with Charlotte. The lights were off, the sunset peeking in through the curtains just enough to keep the room from being completely dark. She held the bed's blanket around her, covering her head and shoulders. She reached up and wiped a tear rolling down her face.

The door opened and closed softly. Charlotte sat next to her on the bed. Lynnette felt her shaking. Her hand slipped from under the blanket and interlocked her pinkie with Charlotte's.

"I don't know what to do," started Charlotte. "I don't know how to feel."

Lynn remained quiet.

"Like, I miss my dad. Even my mom. But... what they did..."

"We don't really know what they did. Not yet."

"They were at least involved. Maybe just as witnesses, but they're connected to it. Somehow. I feel disgusted. Sick."

"It's disgusting but not surprising."

Charlotte's brow furrowed as she turned to face Lynn. "What? What do you mean?"

"I mean your mom has always had a problem with me. With people who look like me. I only knew your dad after the stroke, but he was always kind. I think he was just glad to have someone, anyone, talking to him. But your mom made very little effort to hide how she felt."

"What? No. My parents love you."

"No, they loved your daughter's girlfriend, but they didn't love *me*. They even had a problem with me being their daughter's *girl*friend. You had to have noticed."

"I mean, they're from, like, an older generation. They've had to adjust... to things."

"And I don't?" Lynn let the blanket fall off of her and stood up, facing her girlfriend. "You think I haven't had to adjust to how people look at me, how they treat me just because I'm Black? You're not my first partner, you know. You're not even my first *white* partner. I've gotten looks from people because I kissed you, or just held your hand."

"No. People are different now, or–"

"People are just the same racist fucks they've always been, Charlotte. You just don't notice it because you don't have to."

"Hey!" Charlotte exclaimed, standing and squaring off with Lynn. "I've gotten shit to for being a lesbian, too. Especially down here. You're not my first either, and I've dealt with my own shit."

"I know!" Lynn yelled, then took a breath and placed her hands on Charlotte's shoulders. "I know. But it's different. You may be judged walking around with me, or any other girl, may get called names for it. But on your own, people just see this beautiful white girl. But me? I'm just another Black girl, taking up space they see as belonging to white people. I offend them just by existing and have my entire life."

"I just thought that didn't bother you. I'm not naive, but you've always been so tough."

"Because I've had to be. But I shouldn't have to be."

"But my mom always welcomed you to the house. Always invited you to family meals and holidays. I knew our relationship wasn't what she wanted for me, but she still accepted you. Whenever we'd tell jokes, I know some were kind of racist, but you laughed at those."

"Well, some of them were actually kind of funny. But others just hurt."

"Why didn't you say anything?"

"I shouldn't have had to say anything. But they made you laugh, and I didn't want to be the killjoy."

Charlotte's shoulders dropped. "I'm sorry. Baby, I didn't realize. I'm so sorry."

"How could you realize it? That's just how life was for you. Harmless jokes that made everyone laugh. You didn't have to think about them any deeper than surface level." Lynn sighed and stepped away from Charlotte, crossing her arms and turning away from her. "And your parents, your mom, I'm sure her behavior wasn't new because you started dating me. You've seen her, heard her do and say things your entire life. You're desensitized to it."

"No. My parents have always been respectful of everyone."

"You know your mother has never given me a drink in an actual glass? Not even some cheap Mardi Gras cup. It's always in some disposable plastic cup. Which is exactly how she sees me: disposable."

"I... I never..." Charlotte sat back down on the bed. "I just... I never realized. Fuck. You're right."

"I know I am." Lynn began to pace the bedroom slowly, back and forth. "But what scares me so much right now...is you."

Charlotte's face shot up, staring at Lynn, watching her moving. "What the fuck do you mean you're scared of me?"

"Your parents' fucked up beliefs are deeply rooted. And you've grown up around it. I thought it was just typical, absentminded white privilege but..." Lynn stopped, reached for the blanket and replaced it over her head and shoulders. "Maybe I'm just an idea to you... some way to rebel against casually racist mom and dad. Dating a Black chick, that'll really show 'em!" She turned her back to Charlotte. "Maybe it's not even a conscious thought. Maybe I'm just some fetish for you..."

Lynn turned around and was surprised to see Charlotte standing right in front of her. She hadn't heard her get off the bed. Just as quietly and quickly, Charlotte's arms were around her neck and her face buried in Lynn's shoulder.

"I'm so... sorry..." Charlotte said between sobs. Her whole body was shaking now. Lynn kept holding onto the blanket around her.

Then, it felt like Charlotte's whole body just gave out. Like it was dead weight as she crumbled onto her knees, hands still desperately holding on to her girlfriend. Lynn stood still for a moment, then slowly knelt down and put her arms around Charlotte.

"I'm sorry, Lynn. I'm sorry for this whole fucked up family. You shouldn't have to deal with any of this... I'm sorry this made you feel... feel like..." she couldn't finish. Her words were replaced by heavy sobs.

A soft knock came at the door, and it creaked open; Gordon looked in just enough to meet Lynn's gaze. He had shed his own tears on his round cheeks. Lynn shook her head, and Gordon nodded, closing the door.

"I love you..." whispered Charlotte. Her hold on Lynn grew tighter.

"I know, Charlotte. I love you, too. Things are just... this was a lot to process. For all of us... I think we're both just feeling a little raw right now." She felt Charlotte's face nudging against her shoulder. Then her lips, a soft kiss on her neck, then her cheek. Suddenly their lips were slowly locking together. "No." Lynn was able to blurt out between kisses. She gently pushed Charlotte back. "No. I need time."

"Like... time apart? Away from me?" Charlotte's lips began to quiver.

"No." Lynn leaned forward and wrapped her arms around her girlfriend. "No. I don't want to go anywhere. I don't want you to go anywhere. This is just something we have to take time to figure out..." Her body began to tremble. Then shake. "I don't... I don't want to... want to be some idea to you." Lynn sobbed, falling against Charlotte, crying into the black dress she was still wearing.

"You're not. You're not!" cried Charlotte. "I swear to you. I'm so stupid fucking in love with you, Lynn. With you. With you. With you." Charlotte's brief break from her own crying came to an end, and she joined Lynn. Both sobbing. Both shaking. Holding each other on the floor of their bedroom.

Chapter Five

"I think about killing myself." Gordon hit the back button to rewind the video by a few frames and then hit play.

"At least once a day I think about killing myself. I get these thoughts and just think how easy it would be. Easy to do, and easy to not have to deal with things anymore. I doubt that I will, but I still think about it." He stared at his face in the video, brown hair covered by a blue hat, hazel eyes hidden behind glasses, and a scruffy beard. He always looked shaggy in his videos, no matter how many times he tried to comb his hair and beard.

He sat in front of the computer screen watching his confession play on to the end. He'd been sitting there for the last three hours editing the video, making sure it was ready before uploading it online. Once it was on his video channel, he knew he'd compulsively check the view count every few minutes. He'd done this dozens of times before, but this one was different. Instead of uploading a video reviewing a TV show or movie or video game, he was spilling out his darkest thoughts to strangers on the internet. He'd gotten negative comments before from internet trolls who take joy in belittling people from the safety of their lairs, but he wondered if the comments would be even worse on this video, or at least, *feel* worse. He was exposing himself to that kind of ridicule, always in the hope of a more positive reception.

Once the editing was done he began the upload process, which only consisted of clicking upload and then waiting for however long it took. He took off his glasses and rubbed his eyes, then turned to look at the curled up ball of black fluff in the corner of his apartment.

"What do you think, Bruce? Good video or bad?" he asked the dog. Bruce's response was a loud exhale followed by a stretch into a more comfortable position. "Yeah. I hope it's good, too."

The video finished uploading. Gordon shared it to the usual feeds and websites, and then began his self-torturous waiting game. After five minutes he had one view. After ten, he had two views. After thirty minutes, he had three views. Gordon let out a long sigh, closing the window and exposing his desktop background: three people stood in the picture. An older man wearing a blue baseball cap, with his arms around a young girl and young boy. All three shared the same smile. With a deep sigh, he sorted through the pictures on the laptop and found one of him, Charlotte, and Lynn, making it his new desktop background.

He pushed himself away from his desk and walked a few steps to his bed. The small bed was unmade, sheets and pillows spread between the mattress and the floor. On the table next to it was another baseball cap with his keys, wallet, and electronic cigarette inside it. He picked up the e-cigarette and placed it between his lips, taking a slow drag. The blue light from the e-cig reflected in his glasses. He let out a soft exhale and the vapor drifted lazily from his mouth and filled the small studio apartment a moment before disappearing into the air.

It had been three months since his father's funeral. After spending a month on his sister's couch, he finally had an apartment of his very own in the same building. His desk was covered in various papers, and clothes and unpacked boxes filled the rest of the area. New dog toys and supplies accompanied his new dog, Bruce (an attempt to make the apartment feel less lonely). Charlotte and Lynn had hardly come over to see his new place. Gordon told himself he didn't have them over because of the mess, but he knew that wasn't the only reason.

Gordon turned back to his laptop and opened a new search bar. *Officer Steven Comeaux* he typed. The search turned up older pictures of a man who shared characteristics of the family friend he thought he knew so well. Newspaper articles of arrests he made. Lists of awards given. Only a few mentions of the unsolved murders.

He sighed and reopened the video page and stared at the view count, trying to will it to increase; no such luck. He shook his head, doing his best to put the number of views out of his mind. *It's been thirty minutes. What were you expecting?* He took his blue hat off and swapped it with the hat from the nightstand and pocketed the table's contents, pulling the hat low over his brown hair. He looked at the dog in the other corner of the apartment. "Want to go for a walk?"

Bruce slowly stood up with a long stretch.

"I'll take that as a *yes*."

Gordon stood outside his apartment building, the e-cig between his lips and Bruce's leash wrapped around his wrist. What was once sunny days and sweaty clothes had changed to cooler winds and hoodies. He could see the neighbors walking to and from their own destinations; the windows of most apartments showed signs of Christmas: lights were in the process of being strung up and plastic Santas stood watch. The Christmas spirit wasn't what was going through Gordon's mind when he saw his neighbors preparing for the holidays.

Why would they judge me? They don't know me, Gordon thought, taking another long drag on the e-cig. He looked away from the buildings and down to his dog and watched Bruce perform his usual routine of circling a bush and then relieving himself on it. *I'm sure they have their reasons.*

The next morning, Gordon awoke to the feeling of something walking over his chest. Mornings usually began this way, waking up to Bruce walking on top of him trying to wake him up when it got too late.

"Morning, bud."

Bruce barked right in Gordon's face, then began to lick him repeatedly until he was finally moving. Gordon yawned and reached for his phone, immediately checking to see if his view count had gone up while he was asleep. Before he went to bed he had reached ten views, and now it had gone to fifteen. His views were also joined by a comment waiting for him to read.

> FIRST!

Once he closed the app he checked his two new text messages. One from his sister, Charlotte, and another from Harriet. He read Harriet's first.

> Saw your video. Glad you felt confident enough to put it up. Still meeting this afternoon?

He responded

> Yes

- then put off reading the message from his sister.

He stood up from his bed and opened the bottom drawer of his nightstand. He pulled out a small green bottle with a label on it reading "Prozac 40 MG" and popped the red and green capsule into his mouth, then began the rest of his morning routine. Feed Bruce, then check the view count. Shower, then check the view count. Walk Bruce, then check the view count. By the end of the routine the count had risen from fifteen to eighteen. *Slowly, but surely.*

Charlotte sat on the couch with her girlfriend Lynn and stared at her phone, reading the text she had sent her brother earlier that morning. Her message read "Want to grab lunch tomorrow?" Gordon had yet to reply.

"Just text him again," Lynn said.

Charlotte sighed. "I don't want to be too much of a bother."

"He *needs* someone to bother him," Lynn said as she looked up from her tablet. "You saw his video. He's thinking about killing himself. He needs you to step up and be there for him."

"I guess, but... I don't know how to deal with something like this!" Charlotte cried.

"Who the fuck does? Just text him again and take it from there."

Charlotte nodded and took a deep breath, then thumbed in another message and hit send, then stared at the background of her phone. The image was of her and Lynn. She set her phone to the side and turned to Lynn "He's not the only one dealing with this, you know? He knows I want to be there for him."

"Maybe he doesn't. Your brother's weird that way. He does his own thing on his own." Lynn picked up her tablet again.

"Yeah, but our personal stuff on the internet? It's like he's looking for attention from anyone except me."

"You're both very different people. Not even sure how you're related, but you're both dealing with things in your own way. So you need to figure out the best way to talk to him." Lynn reached over to Charlotte and handed her the tablet. Charlotte looked down at the screen and saw her brother's latest video. Below it was an empty comment box.

Gordon sat across from Harriet, whose outfit was particularly loud, covered with bright red and yellow shapes. Each wrist was covered in wooden bracelets that made this clunking noise every time she moved her hands, and her bright red horn-rimmed glasses were perched in her nest of curly red hair. Her office reflected her personality, with various statues and paintings from different countries and cultures, along with crayon drawings made by some of her younger patients. Normally, someone dressed this loudly would bother Gordon, but they'd had enough sessions that the loud outfits became an endearing trait of hers.

"Any more thoughts?" Harriet asked.

"Yeah. Some." Gordon shrugged, not wanting to look her in the eye. " Like... When I'm driving I wonder about driving off the bridge into the river or walking into traffic."

"Any real desire to do that?"

"No... not really. Just thinking about it. Not trying to do it."

"How do you feel after putting the video up?" she asked, folding her hands into her lap.

Gordon shrugged. "The same... nervous, I guess."

"Nervous about what?"

"Well..." He sat forward in his chair, as if he was telling a secret he wanted no one to hear. "I feel like this video is different. All the others aren't personal. This one is. It's *really* personal. I've gotten bad comments before, but I'm worried about it getting them on this one."

Harriet looked over to the computer on her desk. "Hm. I haven't checked it since this morning. Have you gotten any comments?"

"Not really. Just someone claiming the first comment."

"And how many views?"

"Twenty-two–" Gordon stopped just short — but not short enough.

"I knew you were still counting your views. What have we talked about?" Harriet smiled and shifted her weight.

Gordon sighed, leaning back. "That the view count doesn't matter. As long as I'm enjoying what I'm doing."

"Exactly. Stop worrying about how other people see you and your videos. What matters is how you see yourself and your work. As long as you think it's good, it will be good."

"I just worry that it's not good. I'm trying to make money from these video reviews. The more views I get, the more successful I'm getting."

Harriet laughed. "You knew this was going to be a long road when you began these videos. You did it to help you get your mind off things, right? Making money was just a happy little side benefit that you get to slowly work on. And remember that this video isn't about making money. It's about talking. Getting things off your chest in a place you feel comfortable in. It's not about views or money; it's about you."

The rest of the therapy session was spent with the two of them discussing other events that had happened since they'd last met. Gordon walked back to his car, going through his phone. Two messages were waiting for him, both from Charlotte. The first read:

> Want to grab lunch tomorrow?

And the second:

> Do you want to grab lunch tomorrow?

He let out a heavy sigh as he slid into his car and closed the door. He thumbed into the phone. "Sure."

The drive back home was quick. Bruce got up from his bed in the corner to greet Gordon, then lazily plopped down next to his desk where he knew he could sit. Gordon turned on his computer and immediately went to his video. The view count had passed 30. The first comment had a few likes as well, and he also had another comment waiting.

Your videos fucking suck. You fucking suck. Please fucking kill yourself.

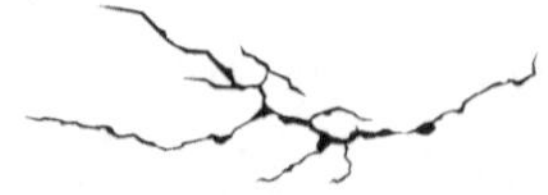

Charlotte stared at her computer, something she'd been doing for the last couple of hours. She'd watched Gordon's video a dozen times now. Her brown eyes and pale cheeks were a bit damp, from a few moments of crying as she watched them. *Dammit, Gordon. Why won't you talk to me?*

She refreshed the video page to watch it again, then noticed a new comment under the first one. "Your videos fucking suck. You fucking suck. Please fucking kill your-self."

What the fuck? What an asshole! She began typing a response to it, full of anger, jumping to the defense of her little brother. She was about three paragraphs in when she stopped. *He doesn't talk to me now... Why would he talk to me after trying to fight his battle for him?* She sighed, erasing everything she wrote. She stared at the empty comment box, *I need to say something.* She began to type.

"At least once a day I think about killing myself. I get these thoughts and just think how easy it would be." Gordon laid in bed, his phone in one hand, Bruce curled up under his other. He ran his fingers through the soft black fur as his eyes focused on the video on his phone.

"Easy to do, and easy to not have to deal with things anymore. I doubt that I will, but I still think about it. My dad... my dad passed away a few months ago. We found out... we uncovered some things about him, and I haven't exactly been dealing with it very well. It wasn't sudden. He was sick for a long time, and then one day I just... I found him and he was gone. We were close. Or I thought we were close. Before that I was dealing with depression, but after... there are days that I have trouble just getting out of bed."

Gordon hit pause on the video and scrolled down to the comments beneath it. He re-read the new comment over and over. "Please fucking kill yourself." Since the comment was left this afternoon, over forty people had liked the comment. *Maybe I should. Not like I'm doing anything worthwhile.*

"No." He shook his head and stood up from the bed, quickly, startling Bruce and sending him scurrying to the edge of the bed. He tossed his phone back on the bed away from him and walked across his room. He grabbed his e-cig and took a long drag, then let the vapor drift lazily from his mouth. He shut his eyes, trying to focus on something else. He felt something walk past his ankle and looked down at Bruce, who was sitting handsomely and looking up at Gordon, which made him smile. Gordon sat down on the floor and pet the small dog, who inched closer and rolled on his back, looking for attention and belly rubs. What else could he do but comply, letting a soft laugh escape him.

"Yeah, Bruce, you know how to make everything about you, don't you."

In agreement, Bruce let out a quick bark and began licking Gordon's hand.

Play time was interrupted by a beep coming from the bed. The phone screen had lit up and vibrated a few times before going silent again. Gordon sighed and stood up, walking back to his bed and looking at the notification. He had a new comment on his video. He hesitated opening it. Probably another nasty one telling him to kill himself. *Maybe they found a more creative way to tell me I suck?* He opened it on his phone and began to read:

> Things really suck, but I know what you're going through. At least I think I do. We all have different problems in our lives, and we deal with them in different ways. I lost my dad too, and I've been trying to stay strong for my family, but... I think I'm mostly trying to stay strong for myself. But knowing that someone else is going through this, I feel less alone. I hope that this helped you as much as it did me listening to you talk.
>
> I've enjoyed your other videos, keep up the good work!

> Also, that guy that told you to kill yourself is an asshole! Fuck that guy!

Gordon looked at it on his phone, reading it over and over again. He eventually put it down and took to reading the comment from his computer. *Someone actually likes my videos?* He read over the comment again. *They're thanking me?* Before he realized it, a smile had taken over his face. He kept reading over the comment for the next hour, watching his video with a brighter outlook. *This helped someone.* It was in a small way, and just that fact, helped him. The views on his video began to rise again, and more and more likes were given to the asshole's comment, but he realized it didn't matter how many views he got because it only took one person viewing it to make a difference for him and a difference for that one person. He stepped away from his computer and went back to the floor to continue playing with Bruce until they both fell asleep, exhausted and content.

The next morning began much like the previous one. Bruce walked on Gordon's chest, barking and licking, trying to wake him up. He pet the small dog and reached for his phone to find one message from Charlotte. "Still on for lunch?" He sighed, not looking forward to talking to his sister, but at the same time, he was not willing to let her spoil his good mood.

A few hours later, Gordon sat across from Charlotte. A basket of cheese fries sat between them. She was wearing her usual big bug-eyed sunglasses that covered half her face. He thought they looked stupid.

"So... How's the job hunt going?" she asked.

Wow. Only took you two questions before you asked about that. "It's going."

"You know," Charlotte started, "I could talk to some friends and see if they know anyone that's hiring."

"No, it's fine." he replied.

"Well, you need to find something. The insurance mon-ey isn't going to last forever."

I have found something... my videos.

Charlotte leaned back in her chair, teasing the salad in front of her with her fork. "So... what's up with that video?"

"What video?" Gordon had a feeling he knew where this might go, but he tried to delay it.

"You know which one. The one you put up the other day about wanting to kill yourself."

Gordon laughed. "Oh, so you do watch my channel. That's sweet of you."

"Shut up, you know that I do. Is that for real? I mean what the fuck, Gordon? You just air our family drama on the Goddamned inter-?"

"I wasn't trying to upset you!" Gordon cut her off. "I was just being honest!"

"Well why the hell couldn't you be honest with me? I try to talk to you all the time and figure out what's going on, but you never tell me anything."

"No, you talk *at* me."

"Fuck you. I try to talk to you, but all you talk about is your stupid hobby and–"

"No! Fuck you! It's not a hobby. This is becoming my job. I am making videos, reviewing movies and shows and giving my opinion, and I'm making money from them! It's not a lot, but it's growing. So give me a Goddamned break! This helps me deal with Dad's death, and it can start helping me financially. So just back off, Charlotte!"

His sister sat across from him, just staring at him. He couldn't see her eyes behind her glasses, but the tears were back. She got up and walked to the bathroom.

Shit, thought Gordon.

Charlotte stood in the bathroom, staring into the mirror. Her glasses were pushed up on top of her long auburn hair and she wiped away her tears with a paper towel. *That went well...* She pulled out her phone and looked at the picture. Her and Gordon were smiling. She smiled back at the picture, pocketed the phone and took a deep breath.

When she walked back to the table, Gordon's back was towards her, and across from him was her empty seat. As she neared the table she got a glance over his shoulder. He was looking at his phone, and in the center of the screen was the comment she had written, unbeknownst to her brother. She did her best to hide a smile as she sat back down. Gordon did the same, switching from his goofy smile quickly to his usual frown.

Gordon started, "Charlotte, I'm..."

"Gordon, I'm sorry. You're not the only one trying to deal with Dad, you know? He died, and we haven't talked to mom and you just shut down... now you *never* talk to me, and I'm just trying to help you. I know you're taking this hard, but... so am I..." She looked at her brother.

He stared at her quietly for a few moments.

"You're right."

"Oh fuck you Gordon, don't patronize–"

"No. Really. You're right. Charlotte. I'm sorry. I didn't think."

"No. You do think but only about yourself sometimes. You get so focused on your own shit that you don't realize how people are feeling around you. I know that's hard with everything, but I'm your sister and you just ignore me like I'm some idiot. I do watch your videos, and I think you say some great stuff. But how was I supposed to know you were making this your job? You never talk to me. I just... I want you to talk to me again."

Gordon sat at his desk, setting up his camera onto a tripod. He'd opened a window to let in some natural light. A knock came from his door, getting Bruce's attention. "Yeah?" Gordon said, still setting up his camera.

The door opened and Charlotte stepped inside. Bruce quickly raced over to her and began circling her, standing on his hind legs.

"I know! I missed you too, Bruce!" said Charlotte, playing with the small black ball of excitement at her feet. She picked up Bruce and cradled him in her arms. "So, this is how you do your videos?" asked Charlotte.

"Yep, record here, then edit, then upload. Easy enough. Just takes a lot of time."

Charlotte nodded, looking at the camera and the computer as Gordon explained. "And... how do you get money from this?"

"Depends on how many views I get, subscriptions, stuff like that. It's not a lot but it's something." Gordon turned his chair to face Charlotte.

"That's actually pretty cool." Charlotte smiled at her little brother.

"And, I was hoping you'd do this video with me."

Charlotte stared at Gordon, her eyes becoming as big as her sunglasses. "Wait, what? Seriously?"

"Yes, seriously, I thought it could be fun," Gordon said, chuckling at her reaction.

"But... But what do I do? I've never done this. Should I be wearing something else? I mean, I'm in a t-shirt and sweatpants! I can't go on camera!"

Gordon laughed, "It'll be fine. We just sit here and talk about stuff." He watched as his sister calmed down, and a smile spread across her face.

"We just... talk?"

Gordon smiled. "Yes. You and me. Just talking."

Charlotte returned the same goofy smile he had. "Sounds good."

Chapter Six

"My doctor's appointment is for two o'clock," Charlotte picked out a cheddar-bacon-ranch covered french fry from the red basket in the middle of the table, then brought it to her mouth and took a bite, slowly chewing, savoring the taste. "So, if you don't mind waiting, it shouldn't take too long."

"Sure. What's the appointment for again?" asked Lynn, grabbing a slightly less covered fry from the same basket

"Just want to go over some lab results from my check-up a couple of weeks ago. Nothing big." Charlotte was mid-chew of the rest of her fry as she picked out another one. "My toes were feeling weird. Going numb and tingling for, like, no reason."

"Does that happen after you've been sitting or laying on them or something?"

"No. It just happens randomly. It's weird. Probably nothing, but that's what check-ups are for. I just..." Charlotte let out a long breath, reaching up and adjusting the large sunglasses on top of her auburn hair. "I just hate going to the doctor. I've gone to enough doctors with my dad to last a lifetime. So, thanks for coming with me."

"No problem. But, your brother couldn't go with you?"

"Gordon hates going to the doctor almost more than I do." She grabbed another fry covered in condiments and brought it to her mouth. She took a bite, then watched as a glob of ranch dripped off the fry and onto her shirt. "Dammit!" Charlotte grabbed a napkin from the table while still holding half the french fry between her lips and dabbed frantically at the staining ranch sauce on her already well-worn t-shirt. "Shit. Shit. Crap. Shit. Crap."

"Will you chill out? You're starting to make a scene." Lynn looked around the partially filled restaurant patio, then forced a smile at the young girl and her mother who looked at them disapprovingly from another table when Charlotte began to curse. After a few seconds, Charlotte only succeeded in smearing the sauce into the collection of the other stains on her shirt. "I should probably get rid of this shirt."

"Probably a good idea," Lynn replied, holding back a laugh. "Ready to go?"

"Yeah," Charlotte sighed, grabbing the last handful of fries and stuffing them into her mouth. They both stood from the table and began their walk to the parking lot, Lynn digging through her purse for her keys and Charlotte licking the cheese and ranch residue from her fingers, then sliding her large, round sunglasses from on top of her head to cover her eyes. "Let's get this over with."

"Ms. Guidry? How are we today?" the doctor asked, extending his hand, the other holding a black, sleek, electronic tablet.

"Doing alright Dr. Raymond." Charlotte shook his hand, then folded her hands together and set them in her lap.

"So..." Dr. Raymond sat in the wheeled-chair across from her and looked down at the tablet. "Thank you for coming by. We just want to go over your test results." Raymond stared down at the tablet for a moment, "Uh huh. Hmm..." then he set it down on the counter, wheeled himself to a cabinet and opened a drawer, reaching in and pulling out a black pouch. He unzipped the sides to reveal a small gray device and an even smaller gray tube. "May I?" He held out his hand to take hers. Charlotte nodded and obliged.

Raymond placed one end of a small gray tube against the tip of Charlotte's index finger, then pushed a blue button on the other end. A sharp pain struck her skin as the needle inside pricked her pointer finger, leaving behind a small drop of red blood. Next, the young doctor picked up the small triangular device with a white paper strip at the bottom of it and placed it against the blood on her finger until it emitted a short beep.

"Here you go," Raymond handed Charlotte a cotton swab to wipe away the blood as he sat back in his chair. Charlotte wiped her finger over and over again, but each time a smaller bead of crimson would begin to appear, until she just held the white cotton over it. She'd helped her dad check his blood sugar numerous times after his right side became paralyzed. Just a quick prick of the finger and then a reading on the monitor. It had been awhile since she'd done it for her father, but the memories were still fresh.

The machine in Raymond's hand beeped again and Charlotte looked towards the doctor. 'Hmm." He turned the device to show Charlotte the electronic numbers 500. "Ms. Guidry, this confirms what we saw on your tests. You're diabetic."

"Huh?" The noise escaped her mouth as she sat there staring at the numbers. Charlotte's eyes shifted slowly from the numbers to Dr. Raymond. She could hear him mumbling something. His lips were moving, his hand gesturing to the numbers and then to her, but she only heard white noise. All she could think of was her father going through this. He didn't take care of himself, and it paralyzed him. Gave him an endless amount of health problems, and she, her brother, her mother — they were there to help him through it. The day he was found slumped over in his chair, she was glad. Glad he was no longer suffering and stuck half-paralyzed in a chair, and glad that she no longer had to take care of him. No more hospitals. No more late night ER visits. No more–

"Ms. Guidry? Charlotte?" Raymond looked concerned. "Do you understand?"

"Yeah. Diabetes. Got to change my diet, eating habits, stuff like that." Her face barely moved as her lips mumbled the words.

"It sucks, sure," Raymond said, "but it's manageable. And you're young. We caught it early, and we can start to take care of ourselves. The first thing we'll need to do is to really start working on losing some weight."

"I'm not fat." Charlotte's arms crossed against her lap, and she held her belly, which felt rounder than usual.

"No, uh." Raymond closed his mouth for a moment and collected his next words. "It's not an issue of being fat or thin. Even thin people are diabetic. But working towards a healthier weight, more proportionate to our bodies, will go a long way in bringing our blood sugar down to normal levels."

Raymond kept using words like "we" and "our," like he'd just been told he has diabetes as well. That all the good foods and drinks he loved were just snatched away from him. Charlotte looked the doctor up and down as he attempted to explain the medication he was putting her on. He was short. Broad shoulders. Thin. The only food he'd have to give up were his sports energy drinks. What did he know?

A lot, probably, thought Charlotte. She'd taken care of herself, for the most part. Sure, she'd eat some cheese fries and other foods and drinks that weren't great, but not *that* much, did she? And she worked out. Did yoga. Walked. But her father had it. Her grandmother had it. It felt that no matter what she did, it was inevitable that she would have it.

"So, I'll send the prescription to your pharmacy, it should be ready by tomorrow. And take this, we have enough of them that we can give them to patients instead of you paying money for one." Raymond held open the small black pack. Inside was the grey tube with the needle, the monitor, and a small pamphlet labeled Log Book. Charlotte stood up from the examining table and reached out for the monitoring pack "And remember. Check your blood sugar every morning and two hours after every meal."

"Yeah. Yeah. Got it."

Charlotte stood in the middle of her bedroom. It was dark, save a dim glow from a street light that crept through the curtains of her window. Her old t-shirt laid on the floor, her pajama bottoms were tossed on the bed, her round sunglasses on top of them. The walls around her had pictures of her with groups of people. Smiling. Laughing.

She looked at her reflection in the full length mirror leaning against her wall. Her eyes scanned her naked body up and down. She turned right and left, examining herself. Her hands ran to her thighs, her arms, then her stomach, squeezing her belly and looking at the chubby skin that half-filled her hands *Fuck.*

She never thought of herself as fat. She was proud of her curves, most days. Or so she told herself. Now, she didn't know how she felt about them. Her mind drifted towards the cheese fries she had for lunch. She tried to remember how they tasted. Instead of memories, her mind flooded with fears of never tasting them again, or soda, or nachos, or rum. *Oh, shit. Rum!* She sighed as the thoughts of her nights drinking with friends came to a halt.

"Charlotte! Time to check your blood sugar!" Her girlfriend's voice came through the closed door. Charlotte sighed and slipped on her pajama bottoms and another t-shirt and shuffled out of her room.

In the kitchen, Charlotte saw the cupboard and pantry doors were open, empty spaces where boxes of food once stood. She found Lynn in front of the open refrigerator, also dressed in her pajamas, her long dark hair tied behind her, and the light of the refrigerator putting a glow on her dark skin. A large trashcan full of food boxes was next to her.

"What are you doing?"

"Getting rid of all the crap we can't eat anymore." Lynn pulled the last few cans of soda out and tossed them in the trash can. Each bang of the can hitting the bottom was like a prick in Charlotte's heart.

The new pack containing the medical device sat on the counter near the sink. Charlotte shuffled over and opened it to find the needle and monitor. Her hands loaded the test strip into the monitor, then cocked back the needle, just like she did for her father. She picked up the gray tube and pressed it to her finger, then pushed the button and felt the sharp prick on her skin. She continued the routine and noticed Lynn watching from behind her.

"Does it hurt?" Lynn asked.

"Kind of. Just for a second." Charlotte typed in the number 476 into a note app on her phone. Next to the number she wrote 'I hate this.' She closed the pack and pocketed her phone, then heard the doors of the refrigerator close.

"So what do we have left?" Charlotte asked.

"Um," Lynn looked around at the now half-empty cupboards. "Wheat bread. Swiss cheese. A bag of almonds. Grilled chicken. And... Water." She forced a smile towards Charlotte. "See? Not all that bad. We can make this work."

Charlotte looked around the half-empty kitchen. "We barely have any food left. We really ate that much crap?"

"I was surprised too. Everything we usually eat isn't great for us, but some things were worse than others. We'll need to go to the store."

"When?"

"Well, unless you want to have grilled cheese for dinner... I'll drive."

Lynn pushed a basket full of boxes and other items, many sporting the label "sugar free," while Charlotte shuffled behind her. They turned down the frozen food aisle, Lynn opened one of the tall glass doors and picked out items. Charlotte stood back, looking at her reflection in the glass. Her shoulders slumped down, making her appear shorter than she was. Behind her reflection was a round tub labeled, "Mint Chocolate Chip Ice Cream."

"Lynn! Can I get this?" asked Charlotte, opening the door and pulling out the tub to show her.

"Is it sugar free?"

"Yes...?" Lynn didn't look back, but Charlotte could feel the disapproving face behind her curly hair.

"Ugh. Fine." Charlotte put the tub of ice cream back into the freezer and continued her shuffle. After a few paces, she turned again to look at her reflection in the glass door. She looked rounder, shorter. She barely recognized herself. She moved on, looking at the food behind the glass, and stopped once again. "Lynn! What about–"

"No."

"You didn't even hear what I was going to say," Charlotte said, pulling out a bright yellow bag with the words "Pizza Rolls!" in large red letters. Lynn sighed and turned around, rolling her eyes as she saw the bag.

"Definitely not."

"So, I basically can't eat anything good?" Charlotte huffed, putting the bag back into the freezer.

"What are you talking about? Look at all the stuff we've already got. It's good for us, and it's actually less expensive. This may not be such a bad thing."

Charlotte caught up with Lynn and rummaged through the basket, pulling out a box labeled Quinoa. "Kee- Keen-KEEN-NO-UH?" Charlotte tried pronouncing the word. "What's Keenouh?"

"KEEN-WAH," Lynn pronounced. "It's a type of rice, I think. But I looked up stuff online, and it's actually good for us."

"Just the sound tastes terrible. KEENWAH!" said Charlotte, frowning as she tossed the box back into the basket.

"If it tastes that bad, we won't get it again. But we have to at least try it. We need to change our eating habits."

"We?"

"Yeah. We can change our diets and eat better and get healthier."

"You're not the one that's diabetic, Lynn. I am. You can eat whatever you want." Charlotte frowned, crossing her arms over her chest and walking ahead of her girlfriend.

"No, I can't. I'm not going to eat all the stuff that you can't anymore. It's a big change, but you're not alone in this."

"Bullshit I'm not."

"It's not the end of the world. It's a manageable condition. A lot of people have this and deal with it. Hell, your brother is probably going to have it. He eats worse than you do."

"Well, I'm not a lot of fucking people, am I?" Charlotte turned around, set her feet and stared at Lynn. "I'm me. I have to deal with this shit. Not you. Not a lot of people. Me. This is my life. And regardless of what I do, I'll probably still end up–" She stopped short before the words left her mouth. She realized her fists were clenched at her side, shaking, her face was feeling hot, her eyes wet. "Give me your keys."

Lynn looked down quickly, hiding her face from Charlotte. She grabbed her purse and pulled out her keys and held them out, stifling a quiet whimper. Charlotte snatched them from her hand and walked towards the front of the store. The aisles passed her quickly, other shoppers, check-out lines, doors, empty carts, until she was sitting in the passenger seat of Lynn's car. Leaning her head against the window, she looked into the side view mirror. Instead of her body and her flabby skin in the reflection, she saw herself in a chair, her right side slumped over.

A knock at her door. Small shafts of sunlight broke through the closed curtains. A second knock. Charlotte rolled over in her bed, facing away from the door and pulling the covers over her head. A third knock.

"I only knocked to be polite. I'm coming in. Better be decent." Charlotte heard the door open and loud footfalls heading towards her bed. "Come on, Charlotte. Get up,"

Gordon sighed loudly. The mattress shifted as he sat down on the bed. "Charlotte."

"What?"

"You okay?"

"What do you think?" She pushed the covers away from her head and looked at her brother. Her eyes quickly scanned his face and body, his long brown hair under his usual blue baseball cap, chubby cheeks, glasses, scruffy brown and red beard, chubby belly. *Guess you're next, little brother.*

"Yeah, Lynn told me." Gordon laid down next to his sister, putting his hands behind his head and leaned back on a pillow.

Charlotte could hear her fan and the air conditioner, Gordon's breathing next to her. Other than that, there was silence.

"I don't..." Charlotte managed to get those two words out. There was no movement from Gordon. He just laid there next to her, still. Charlotte shifted to lay on her back, bringing her hands in front of her face and picking at her nails. "I don't want to... I don't want to end up like Dad."

"I have that same fear everyday of my life." Gordon let out a long sigh. "But you're not. And neither am I."

Charlotte turned her head to look at her brother. He still hadn't moved, hadn't changed his focus from staring up at the ceiling.

"Dad was diagnosed with diabetes years ago," Gordon began. "He didn't do anything about it. He kept eating the way he did. He still lost his temper and got overstressed. It took him three heart attacks and a stroke before he got the message that he needed to take care of himself, but by then, it was too late." Gordon took a deep breath. "But you know now. It's two-thousand-fucking-twenty-five. They have medicine and ways to manage it. And you already make at least an effort to take care of yourself."

Gordon was right. *Of course he's right.* Charlotte didn't want to tell him that. It'd go to his head if he ever heard those words come out of her mouth. But she couldn't help but crack a quick smile. She continued picking her fingernails and nudged his side with her elbow. "Love you, little brother," she mumbled.

"Yeah, I know." Gordon stood up from the bed and pulled the covers away from Charlotte. "Now get up. I have a doctor's appointment in an hour and you're coming with me."

"The fuck I am," said Charlotte, turning back onto her side.

"Yeah, you are. I need to check myself, see if I'll have to suffer with you or not." Gordon walked to the windows and threw open the curtains. A burst of sunlight filled her room. She cowered from it, curling into a ball. "I'm dragging your dumb ass with me one way or another." He laughed, picking up her large sunglasses from her nightstand and tossing them to her. "Plus, I bet you twenty bucks my blood sugar score is lower than yours." Charlotte looked at him from under the pillow.

"Fuck. Fine!"

"Dammit!"

Charlotte slammed the front door behind her, clenching her fists and stomping her feet. Lynn peeked her head out from the kitchen to see the commotion. "What the hell?"

"Four seventy! Four! Seventy!" Gordon smirked and raised his fists into the air, walking towards Charlotte's couch and taking his throne like a king. Charlotte pulled her keys from her pocket and threw them across the room, narrowly missing Gordon and hitting a couch cushion.

"Four seventy what?" asked Lynn, tilting her head and raising her eyebrows.

"Gordon's stupid blood sugar! It was four seventy. Mine was five hundred. His was lower, and now I'm out twenty bucks. Ugh. I hate you!"

"I know you're a little strapped for cash so I'll give you twenty-four hours to come up with my money, or I break your kneecaps." Gordon winked, then quickly curled into a ball on the couch as Charlotte lunged for him, grabbing a pillow and hitting him with it repeatedly. "A little help?" Gordon called to Lynn between Charlotte's attacks. Lynn laughed and shook her head, ducking back into the kitchen.

"Wait..." Charlotte paused her attack. A subtle, nutty smell was filling the apartment, and whatever it was, it smelled good. "What are you cooking?" Charlotte tossed the pillow back on top of her brother, who was already getting comfortable and looking at his phone.

Lynn stood by the stove, moving a wooden spoon around a skillet full of bits of brown rice and dark specks of something Charlotte didn't recognize. "It's the quinoa we got last night," said Lynn, staring intently down into the skillet.

"The keen- oh…" Charlotte followed the movements of the spoon against the black surface of the skillet. "Lynn… I'm…" Charlotte took a deep breath. "I'm sorry. I was an ass last night."

"Yeah, you were." Lynn looked up and smiled. "It's alright."

"But… Why are you doing all this? I told you, this is my problem, you can eat however you like."

"No." Lynn sighed and set down the spoon, turning to face Charlotte. "It's not *your* problem. It's *our* problem. You were there for your dad through this. Both of you." Lynn shifted her gaze momentarily to Gordon laying on the couch, who quickly turned his attention back to his phone, as if he wasn't paying attention. "And now I'm here for you. And I could stand to be healthier, so it works out."

Charlotte smiled, then leaned into Lynn and wrapped her arms around her. "Thank you." Lynn returned the embrace. After a moment, the hug ended, and Charlotte stepped back, wiping something from her eyes.

"Well, this is awkward," said Gordon, loudly.

"Shut up, Gordon." Lynn grabbed the empty Quinoa box on the counter and threw it at him, "Oh no, I needed that for the cooking directions."

"Ugh. Dammit." Lynn turned to see Charlotte facing the skillet, holding the wooden spoon near her mouth. "This... is actually pretty good."

Lynn let out a sigh of relief as she walked the length of the apartment to retrieve the cardboard box. When she turned back towards the kitchen, Charlotte was leaning against the counter staring at her. "Why are you doing all this?"

"Why am I doing all what?" asked Lynn as she returned to stirring the rice and quinoa.

Charlotte gestured to the stove and then around the kitchen to the half empty cabinets. "I told you, I'm the one who needs to change and eat differently. Not you."

"Because I love you, dumbass. You're not alone. And it won't kill me to eat healthier. Quite the opposite actually."

Charlotte began wringing her hands together, shifting her weight from one foot to the other. "Hold that thought." She ran from the kitchen and into their bedroom. After a moment she remerged, and she was much more hesitant walking towards Lynn, holding something small in her hands.

"I... I don't deserve you."

"Yes you do–" Lynn tried to cut in.

"No. Let me get this out." Charlotte took a deep breath. "I don't deserve you. Especially these last few months. You've been my rock when you didn't have to be. You kept me balanced and I... I've had a lot to process. You've given me the support and patience I needed, and you still go above and beyond to love me... and I love you so fucking much." Charlotte paused, then shakingly got down on one knee.

"Oh shit." Gordon muttered from the sofa, then quietly slipped out his phone and pointed the camera lens towards Charlotte and Lynn.

"This is dumb." Charlotte shook her head then stood up and held out a small, velvet box towards her hopefully new fiancé. "Lynn... Will you marry me?"

A small clatter came from the frying pan as the wooden spoon fell from Lynn's hand. She stared wide eyed as Charlotte opened the ring box, revealing a golden band with a single diamond embedded in the center.

"This is... this is just because you lost your dad," rationalized Lynn while her eyes began to tear up.

"No. I bought the ring a long time ago. I was going to propose sooner, but then everything happened. I couldn't be more sure about this decision than I am right now."

Lynn let out a brief sob, then with shaking hands reached for the box. She slowly lifted the golden band from its nest and stared at it. She then handed the ring to Charlotte. "Yes. Yes. Yes!"

Charlotte cried out as her hand joined with Lynn's around the ring. She took it and gently slid it onto her future wife's finger.

"Woohoo!" yelled out Gordon, standing from the couch.

Charlotte laughed and embraced Lynn, kissing her once, twice, three times as they held each other tight.

"Gross. Get a room, you two!"

"Shut up, Gordon!" Charlotte and Lynn shouted in unison as Lynn, again, threw the quinoa box at her future brother-in-law.

Part Three

Chapter Seven

Officer Sarah Bennett had been off her shift for fifteen minutes. She still wore her uniform, various tools attached to her belt and pockets. Sitting at a dark green metal table on the front porch of the cafe, she tapped on her phone. She pressed various shapes and colors, collapsed rows on top of themselves, and reached for a large plastic cup of frozen coffee with whipped cream and chocolate drizzles and took a long sip from the straw.

The sun had set, leaving the sky a cloudy light blue, and the only lights were a few twinkling string lights, and the neon sign that read, "Coffee House" hanging from the red brick wall.

A hand grabbed the dark green metal chair across from her. "Officer Bennett?"

Sarah looked up from her phone and saw a short man, about her own height, maybe an inch taller, with shaggy brown hair and a beard, his glasses pushed up to the top of his nose. "Mr. Guidry." She stood up and shook his hand, then gestured to the chair. "Please, have a seat."

Gordon pulled out the chair and sat down, setting a thick manilla envelope in front of him on the table. "Thank you for meeting with me."

"My pleasure. I was surprised to get your call. It's been a few months since your father passed. How have you and your family been doing?" She asked out of a sense of politeness, *but the circles under your hazel eyes? They tell me everything I need to know.*

"Um... as best as we can, given the circumstances." Gordon tapped his fingers quickly against the metal table, causing a small, repetitive clanging sound. To Sarah, he looked like he was deciding whether or not to confess to something.

"You mentioned you had some more information about your father?"

His fidgeting stopped, then started back up again. "Uh. Yeah. Yeah..." He reached for the envelope, then quickly took his hand back as if afraid of being bit. "Um. We found something. Going through my parents' things." He reached again for the envelope and slowly opened it. He turned the envelope upside down and poured out its contents; a few photographs, a newspaper clipping, a white piece of cloth, and a small silver ring.

"May I?" She paused briefly and waited for Gordon to nod his head before picking up the photo. She flipped it over to read the back. Her eyes focused on the names, then turned the photo again. "Is that...?" She stared at the younger versions of faces she'd seen before. *That asshole.*

"My mother, my father, and Steven Comeaux, a family friend."

"I'm familiar with Officer Comeaux." His name left a bad taste in her mouth. She set down the photo, face down on the table, then read the news clipping, then examined the cloth, a mask as it turned out, and the ring.

"We found these with my parents' things. With the photo and the newspaper clipping, we think that it might connect my parents and Steven to the murder."

"That's a bit of a leap, if I'm being honest, Mr. Guidry."

"Just Gordon, please."

"Gordon." She nodded, reading the clipping. "The photo of Steven isn't surprising. Between you and me, he's always been an ass, so being involved with the klan is practically old news. And just because his father was tied to the investigation doesn't say much. Comeaux Senior made his way pretty high up the ranks. He was in charge of a lot of investigations."

"Then why was *this* clipping saved with this photograph?!" Gordon asked, leaning forward and pointing at the photograph of his parents.

"That's what we would need to figure out." She looked at Gordon. His face was tense, as if holding something back. *Is he going to cry? Oh, boy...*

Sarah leaned back and gave Gordon a moment to compose himself. "Would you like something to drink, Gordon? A coffee? Some water?" Gordon shook his head and leaned back in his chair. Sarah nodded. "Okay, Gordon, I want you to lead me through your thought process on this. How you found these, and why you think this all connects them to a murder." Sarah grabbed the notepad and pen from her front pocket.

Gordon took a deep breath. "After my dad died, I was going through all of their finances. Steven came over and seemed interested in this particular envelope. He seemed *very* interested in it. So I looked through it and found this. I wasn't sure what the clipping meant, but the photograph was pretty damning. At the very least, it shows my parents were involved with... with the klan." Gordon began to shake.

"Take your time, Gordon." Sarah stopped writing for a moment.

"So I brought these to my sister, and we talked about them. I thought the clipping was important. Why else would they save it if they weren't connected to it? Why would Steven want it so badly? We looked up the whole article online, more than the clipping said, and as far as we could tell, the murder has been left unsolved. So with Steven's father being a cop at the time, we thought maybe he had a way to cover it up, clean up his son's and his friends' involvement."

Sarah continued writing in her pad, then turned to a fresh sheet. She took a breath and set the pad and pen down and looked at Gordon. "I hate to say this, Gordon, but none of this is damning evidence. It's circumstantial at best, and even that is a stretch. The photo could be explained as an awkward photo taken in the wrong place at the wrong time. And the only connection we have between the photo and the article is Steven's father being in charge of the investigation."

"But the mask? The ring?"

"Don't mean much if we don't know for sure where they came from. And even then, it might just be guilt by association, which doesn't amount to much, if anything. Unless we have hard evidence connecting them to the crime, a murder weapon, DNA, something tangible, this doesn't do much. This isn't like a detective movie where the pieces just fit together, and we arrest the bad guy."

Gordon's mouth opened and closed, looking for words that just wouldn't come.

"I know that's not what you wanted to hear. But..." *I shouldn't say this.* "I do believe you, or at least think you're on the right track." Sarah began collecting the items and replacing them into the envelope. "What I can tell you is that there's already plenty to suspect about Comeaux. The few times I've worked with him, his arrests aren't usually clean, especially with Black suspects. He's rougher than is ever necessary. He's racked up plenty of complaints. But most of those are either handled quietly, or they are just swept away."

Gordon finally sat back in his chair, sinking into it as if he were a deflating balloon.

I wish I had better news, Gordon.

Some hours had passed since Sarah met with Gordon. Now, instead of the shaggy haired man sitting across from her, she faced a laptop screen. Where earlier, she'd worn a uniform with her hair tied up in a ponytail, she now sported pajama shorts and a tank top, her hair falling down to her shoulders. Gordon's envelope sat beside her on her desk, opened with the photo and clipping laying in front of it.

Sarah typed into the laptop and brought up the full article online. In the window next to it she had the original scanned police report. Gordon was right, the case had remained unsolved, no suspects, and honestly there was hardly an investigation at all. *You're probably right, Gordon. I wish you weren't.*

She wrote a few more notes onto her pad, then picked up the photo. Steven, Dean, and Jeanine stared at her with the bright flash of the fiery cross behind them. The photo made her want to gag. *I can't imagine how this made you feel,* she thought, thinking of Gordon sitting across from her at the cafe, shaking, looking as if he were about to let out three months worth of tears.

The least I can do is ask around.

"He confessed?" asked Gordon, his eyes wide.

"He did," responded Sarah, leading Gordon and his sister through the back halls of the police station. Under the fluorescent lights, they walked past other officers in similar uniforms to Sarah's. Reaching the end of the hall, they reached a metal door. Through the door's small rectangular window they could see Steven Comeaux sitting at a large metal table. His hands were on top of the table in handcuffs.

He used to be so big. He looks so small now, thought Gordon.

"I wasn't sure it would do anything," started Sarah, "but I brought what you gave me to internal affairs. They began to look into it and as soon as Comeaux caught wind of it, he came in and confessed."

"That son of a bitch," said Charlotte, grabbing Gordon's arm. He could feel her nails digging into his skin.

"He's asked for his lawyer and to speak with you. I can give you a few minutes with him," continued Sarah, opening the door and gesturing inside.

Gordon could feel the perspiration forming on his forehead, his hands beginning to sweat as he and Charlotte sat across the table from the cop they'd known their whole lives. Steven tried smiling at them, but what he must have thought would come off as a comfort, just looked sad, like a king knocked off his throne.

"I'm, uh, glad to see ya' both. How've you been since, well, since the funeral. I know your mama misses you something fierce..."

"Shut the fuck up about her you piece of shit," interrupted Charlotte. Gordon could see the stern expression on her face. Her hand was still holding his arm, her grip tightening even more.

"I just, hmm, I just wanted to clear the air for you," continued Steven.

It can't be this easy, thought Gordon. He remained quiet, waiting for Steven to do what he thought was clearing the air.

"First off, I wasn't alone, but I had a hand in killin' that man. Not your folks. My daddy, me, and others, but they're all long gone now. So it's just me left to take the blame. But yo' mama and daddy never had no part in it."

"The picture?" asked Charlotte.

"Hmm, my daddy had been a part of a group. He brought me into it when I was 16. I was young and dumb. Been in it a year when I convinced your daddy to join me at our meetings. He'd come to a few here and there, got excited about what they'd be sayin', but never went no further than that. One night, he brought your mama to a meeting. That's when the picture was taken. She never came to any others. Your daddy only came to a few more after that." He stopped and cleared his throat. "So, I'm, uh, I'm tellin' you this so you know your folks were better people than you're thinking they are. They never did any of the things I was involved with. Just some meetings. So, uh, yeah, now you know, and maybe you can forgive your mama.”

They sat in silence for what felt like hours. The only noise was the occasional rattle of Steven's handcuffs, and the tick tick ticking of a clock. Then the scraping of Charlotte's chair as she got up and knocked on the door. Sarah opened it quickly and let Charlotte out. Gordon turned and met Sarah's eyes, then nodded. She closed the door and left them both back in the silence. "Why are you telling us this?" asked Gordon.

"I've done a lot of bad things, kid. But losin' your daddy... he was my brother. I ain't got no other family than him, and your mama and you and your sister..."

"You think we're family?"

"I hoped... I never meant to hurt y'all. I never meant to hurt your family. Maybe makin' this right is the last thing I can do for Dean, puttin' your family back together."

Gordon let out a quick laugh, then shut his mouth tight. "You..." he started, then stopped. The tick tick ticking was growing louder as they sat in silence. "You're not the one that broke this family. And you're sure as shit not the one who can ever put it back together." Gordon stood and knocked on the door.

Charlotte lurched over the porcelain bowl and wretched her stomach's contents into the water. She took a breath then wretched again and again. Finally her stomach stopped doing somersaults, and she slowly stood up, holding onto the stall door for support. She kicked the flusher with her foot and wiped her mouth. Opening the door, she saw she wasn't alone. Sarah leaned against the row of sinks across from the bathroom stalls, holding out a thin stack of paper towels.

"Thanks."

"No problem," responded Sarah.

Charlotte stepped to a sink next to Sarah and began using a towel to wipe her mouth before washing her hands. She then cupped her hands and filled them with water, taking a sip and swirling the water in her mouth, then spit it out.

"That water's probably not good for you," suggested Sarah.

"I've had worse."

"At the risk of asking a really stupid question," started Sarah. "Are you okay?"

Charlotte looked Sarah up and down. *She's cute,* thought Charlotte. *Pretty eyes.* "I'm as good as I'm gonna be, I guess."

"Did anything he said help? Maybe make things easier to deal with?"

"What, instead of being a shitty racist murderer, my parents are just shitty racists?"

"Fair point," responded Sarah. "Is there anything I can do to help, for you or for Gordon?"

"I think putting that piece of shit in prison is the best you can do." Charlotte dried her hands and threw away the paper towels. "But the damage has already been done."

Gordon leaned against the wall near the bathrooms. *I had so much to say,* he thought. *Why didn't I yell? Scream? That was my chance, and I just... I barely said anything.* The door with the plastic woman sign on it opened, and Sarah stepped out. When she saw Gordon waiting there, she nodded and joined him leaning against the wall.

"Thank you for this," said Gordon.

Sarah nodded again. "I just hope this gives you at least some sort of closure, at least on this."

"I don't know that it does." Gordon sighed and shrunk down on the ground, still leaning against the wall. Sarah joined him at the same level. "Our parents are still... what they are. What they were."

"They're still your parents, though, right?"

"Yeah... but this changes so much about them."

"Does it?"

Gordon turned and faced Sarah.

She'd crossed her arms on her knees and rested her head, staring forward. "I've seen a lot of tragedy here. A lot of loss. Most of it is senseless. But what I've learned is that there's no one or the other. No black or white. No blanket statements. People are messy and complicated. People can be two things... your parents were a part of some awful things, and even today, probably still have those beliefs. But they were also your parents, and considering how you seem to have turned out, they were probably pretty good parents. As good as they could be anyway." She turned and noticed Gordon watching her. She reached over and squeezed his hand. "Give yourself a break on this. You and your sister both. Stop trying to fit your parents into one camp or another. They're racist. But they're also your parents. One doesn't change the other." Gordon squeezed her hand back. "Just my two cents, is all."

"And the family of the man Steven killed? Do they get closure?" Gordon asked, feeling guilty about all the focus being on his feelings and his loss.

"They get to know that at least one person will face judgement for the murder. It isn't a lot, but it's something," Sarah said, her voice soft.

"Seems to be a lot of that going around." Gordon frowned.

"I told you this wasn't a detective movie, Gordon. There's no real justice when one person kills another. There are penalties, punishments, but that man is still dead. Nothing you and I can do will bring him back."

Gordon could only nod in response.

Chapter Eight

"We meet on neutral ground, alright? The park by the river, The Fly," said Charlotte, handing the phone back to Gordon.

"Agreed. We let her say her piece, take it from there." Gordon stared at the phone screen. Against the dark screen was a blue box.

From mom:

> *Can we please talk? There's so much I need 2 say*

Gordon sighed and responded.

> *Tomorrow. Noon. The Fly.*

He turned the phone off and slid it back into his pocket. "Maybe we should go into this with an open mind? Give her a chance?"

"Ha! We're not the ones with closed minds here."

"Yeah, I know, but... I don't know. Steven said she and dad weren't a part of that murder. They just–"

"They just what?" interrupted Charlotte. "Just went to klan rallies? Just treated people — people we love as lesser beings?"

Gordon leaned back in the metal chair and covered his face with his hands. "You're right." His hands slid down his face then arms dropped to the sides of the chair. "She's just... she's still Mom, you know?"

"Yeah, I know." Charlotte took a long drag from Gordon's e-cigarette. "I know." Vapor drifted up lazily into the cloudy sky.

The rain cleared up the next day. Only a few clouds traveled across the sky, occasionally passing in front of the sun. A small tug boat floated down the river as young college students stood on the grassy bank, playfully throwing stones into the water.

Jeanine was already seated at a picnic table when they arrived, a large black binder on the table next to her. She smiled and waved at them enthusiastically as they approached, then wiped at her eyes. Their mother hadn't changed much in the months since the funeral. Thinner maybe. A few more strands of gray in her brown hair.

"Oh! I'm so happy to see you both!" Jeanine gave Gordon a quick hug, then turned to her daughter. Charlotte's eyes went wide as Jeanine squeezed her tight.

"Alright, Ma. Good to see you, too," Charlotte managed to get out as her mother's hug cut off her air supply.

Jeanine relinquished her grip and gestured to the picnic table.

"Sit! Sit! Oh, I was so happy to hear about the engagement! I wish you would have told me instead of me finding out through social media."

"How did you see my announcement?" asked Charlotte, tilting her head and squinting her eyes. "We're not connected there."

"Oh, well, one of the ladies from church saw it and asked me about it. Put me on quite the spot to not know about my own daughter's engagement," said Jeanine as she pressed her lips together and looked at Charlotte with squinted eyes.

"Well, that's your own fault, Ma," responded Charlotte, sitting cross legged on the picnic bench. Gordon sat beside her, straddling either side of the bench to face his family.

"Excuse me?" Jeanine said, leaning back in her seat. "I'm not the one who hasn't answered calls and texts. I've been trying to talk to you both for months!"

"And why do you think that is?" asked Gordon.

"I know this business with Steven has been confusing for everyone. But he confessed. You know that. And now, with that behind us, we can focus on being a family again. We can talk about this wedding you're about to have!" Jeanine smiled and reached across the table for Charlotte's hands but missed as Charlotte recoiled. "Well, anyway." Jeanine reached for the black binder and began flipping through pages. "I got this from the church, I've already spoken with them about potential dates."

"Dates?" asked Charlotte, her eyebrows rising.

"For the big day! They have a few options on how they can arrange the chapel, and what flowers you can use. I wasn't sure what colors you and Lynn might want to go with, so I brought a few ideas."

"You think we're going to get married at your church?"

"Well, of course! Where else? Now, are you going to be wearing the dress, and Lynn, I suppose, will be wearing a pants suit?"

"No... we're both wearing dresses... and we're not getting married at the church, Ma. We booked a venue downtown."

"Oh, I know downtown is hip for you, but you'll regret it, I know. A traditional wedding is definitely the way to go, however untraditional the marriage."

"Excuse me?" reacted Charlotte, wide eyed.

"What, dear?"

"I don't want that. *We* don't want that. We've planned this wedding. It's *our* wedding. Not your ideal traditional wedding. It's going to represent us, and the last thing that represents us is your ideas and your church. I just... I can't believe this. Is that all you wanted to talk about, Ma? The wedding?" asked Charlotte.

"Well, what else is there to talk about?" Jeanine's brow furrowed as she looked between her children.

"How about your involvement with Steven and the klan? The fact that you were holding on to that stuff in the first place? I don't ever want to step foot back in that house knowing it was there," said Charlotte, waving her hands in front of her.

"I think you're making a bigger deal out of this than–" started Jeanine.

"No she's not!" cut in Gordon. "Yeah, Steven cleared things up. You only went to one meeting. Why? It seemed like a fun thing to do on a Friday night?"

"Don't you take that tone with me, Gordon."

"I'll take whatever tone I fucking need to take to get through to you!"

"Gordon, it was a different time. Things were changing, and there were a lot of people that didn't think they were changing for the better."

"Like you?"

"No, of course not... It was just... It was complicated."

"Complicated," Charlotte said as a laugh escaped her. "No, it's pretty simple, Ma. It doesn't matter what time it was. That kind of shit is not okay. Not then, and not now.

Nothing excuses how you and Dad, how we've all acted growing up."

"Well, you never said anything then, I don't see why it's such a big deal now," said Jeanine, crossing her arms over her chest.

"It should have been a big deal then. We were just so used to seeing it and hearing it from y'all that we never really knew what you were saying. What we were hearing." Charlotte wiped a tear from her face, then slid her sunglasses to shield her eyes.

"This is all because of Lynn, isn't it? When have I ever treated her with anything other than love and respect?"

"Any time you told us racist jokes. You may not have been saying them about her, but they still hurt her. Or how you serve her food, on paper plates and plastic cups, like all of a sudden we don't have real plates and glasses. And I'm the bigger fool for not even realizing it."

"Now, hold on, Charlotte, I was just trying to make less work for me when I wash the dishes–"

"Bullshit!" yelled Gordon. "You're not stupid, Ma. You know exactly what you've done, and you know it's unacceptable."

"Oh, everything is unacceptable these days. Can't tell a joke, every word is judged and taken out of context. And now my own children are using my words against me. You both need to understand that things were different when we were growing up–"

"I understand perfectly, Ma. I understand that you've been alive a lot longer than us, and you haven't learned a fuckin' thing."

"You may kiss the bride!"

Charlotte smiled and grabbed Lynn, dipping her and kissing her fiercely. Music began playing and the small audience clapped and whooped and hollered, throwing up white streamers into the air around the newlyweds. Charlotte laughed as she finally let go of Lynn, looking around at everyone and wearing the biggest grin Gordon had ever seen on her face. Her smile reached her eyes, no sunglasses to hide it. As the music crescendoed, the couple walked down the aisle, shaking friends' hands and hugging loved ones.

Seats were rearranged and a dance floor appeared, and Gordon watched as his sister had a simple first dance with his new sister-in-law. As more dancing ensued and cake was cut, Gordon stepped outside on the balcony. He watched the sun set, covering the French Quarter in a soft glow. He watched as people beneath him walked to and from bars, restaurants, and tourist shops.

"Hey."

Gordon turned and saw a woman walking towards him. She wore a blue dress, and the usual bun of her hair was replaced by flowing locks dropping just past her shoulders. "Officer Bennett. I wasn't sure you were going to make it." She held up two flutes of bubbling champagne.

"It's just Sarah, here. I almost didn't make it. I was sitting in the back. Drink?"

"Yes, please." Gordon accepted the glass, their fingers brushing against each other briefly. "Thank you."

"Um, it was a beautiful ceremony."

"It was. Just how they wanted it."

"Hmmmm. I, uh, didn't see your mother," Sarah said as she absentmindedly tapped the stem of her glass.

"And you won't." Gordon took a swig of his drink. "We're going through some family problems."

"Oh, I'm sorry to hear that."

"Thanks. It was suggested we go to family therapy. We're trying to convince our mother to go."

"I can't imagine that will be easy."

"That's an understatement."

Sarah drank from her glass then returned to tapping it with her forefinger. "It's a beautiful day."

"It is." Gordon smiled and nodded.

"I'm sorry, I don't know what to talk about at weddings... or parties... or most social interactions. I'm more used to interrogating someone than just having a conversation."

"I don't think I'd mind an interrogation by you." Gordon laughed, taking another drink. "But you can relax, I'm the awkward one in the family. I have no idea how I'm supposed to act here or anywhere."

"Um, maybe we can figure that out together?"

"I'd be game." He met her smile with his own.

"Oh my God!" Charlotte screamed from the glass doors of the balcony. Gordon turned and saw his sister making her way over, Lynn doing her best to keep up in her heels. Charlotte on the other hand had switched her high heels for sneakers. "You look gorgeous! What are you two talking about out here?" slurred Charlotte.

"I think what my wife means to say is 'Thank you for coming, your dress is lovely.'" Lynn translated for Sarah, finally catching up.

"How much has she had to drink?" asked Gordon as he accepted Charlotte's hug.

"Only, like, one or two glasses of champagne," said Charlotte, moving from Gordon to wrap her arms around Sarah.

"But she hasn't eaten anything all day," Lynn said, reaching out for Charlotte to steady her and lead her to the balcony's railing.

"Let me see if I can grab you some food. You both wait here." Sarah broke away and headed inside, before turning around. "And Gordon, maybe find me on the dance floor later?"

"I will." Gordon raised his glass to Sarah and watched her disappear into the crowd.

"Y'all gonna fuck," said Charlotte, breaking the brief silence.

"Mmmhm," agreed Lynn.

"Stop it, both of you." Gordon blushed and turned to lean against the railing, finishing off his drink.

"You better not screw that up. She comes with handcuffs, if you know what I mean," said Charlotte as she nudged her younger brother.

"We all know what you mean." Lynn reached for Charlotte and held her in a tight embrace.

"I miss Mom and Dad," Charlotte blurted out, followed by a sniff.

"I'm sorry, Charlotte," Lynn responded, running her fingers through Charlotte's auburn hair.

"No, don't be sorry. They need to be sorry. It's their fault. I just..." Charlotte moved from Lynn and joined her brother leaning against the railing. "I don't miss *them*. But I do. I miss parts of them. Ma' would have helped with my dress, and by now, probably running around obsessing over the cake and the catering. And Dad was the social butterfly. Even after the stroke..."

"Yeah... he was good at things like this." Gordon shifted to the side and leaned against Charlotte. "It's okay to miss parts of them. This is a big day."

"It is weird, them not being here. I always imagined..." Charlotte shook her head and turned to Lynn, grabbing her and pulling her to her side, then wrapping her arms around Gordon and Lynn. "What matters is who *is* here. This is the family I want to spend my days with."

"This is weird. Why are you being gushy like this?" asked Gordon, laughing at his drunk sister.

"Hey, shut up! It's my wedding day! I can be as gushy and thoughtful as I want to be!"

Epilogue

The face of the house was small, but looking around the corner, Gordon saw how far back it went, ending in a backyard. The panels of the walls were bright green with flowers painted along the side. A tall woman in paint-stained overalls stood facing the wall, a brush in her hand, moving it gracefully along the surface, bright colors following its movements.

"That looks really beautiful," called Charlotte. The woman's brush stopped and she turned to stare at Gordon and Charlotte standing just beyond the waist high fence.

"Why, thank you!" She set down the brush on the sheet she was standing on and approached them. "Just my own little home improvement project."

"I love it!" exclaimed Charlotte, raising her sunglasses off her face and staring at the paintings.

"We were looking for Jocelyn Harris," said Gordon, smiling at the woman.

"Oh, I just go by Josie. How can I help you?" She stretched out her dark-skinned hand and shook Gordon's fair one.

"I'm Gordon Guidry, that's my sister Charlotte. We, uh, we were hoping to talk to you about your grandfather, Robert Harris."

"Oh! Oh, well, he died before I was born, my grandmother, too. Never had the chance to know them, but Mama and Daddy would talk about them all the time." Josie's gaze drifted for a moment, a small frown forming on her face, looking past Gordon. She shook her head and smiled.

"Josie... We've discovered some things about our parents..." Gordon began to tell Josie about what they'd discovered, the pictures, the murder of her grandfather, Steven Comeaux and his father-

"Stop." Josie raised her hand in front of Gordon. "Just... stop." The smile had faded from Josie's lips, now pressed into a thin line. "Young man, I appreciate why you're here. I do. But you need to understand. You have come to my home and brought up a tragic past that my family has long since buried."

Gordon blinked. "I'm sorry. I thought-"

"You thought what?" interrupted Josie. "You thought you would bring me closure? You thought I have been waiting all my life to know what happened to my grand-daddy? My family always knew what happened to him. He was taken from us by pure hatred. That is something my family struggles to come to terms with everyday, and it doesn't matter that someone is in jail for his murder now. I don't accept your closure, and I have no forgiveness to give you if that is what you're seeking. Please, Gordon, please go." Josie took a deep breath, then turned and walked inside her home, the paints and brushes discarded in the yard.

Minutes later, Charlotte and Gordon sat in his car as he drove them home. The sun was still shining, but rain had begun to fall. The light coming towards him changed from green to yellow then red and his foot gently pressed the break. A tall, thin man with patchy gray hair and dark skin stood up from the bucket he was sitting on under an overpass to stay out of the rain and held up a sign that read "Any help is a blessing." He gave a crooked but genuine smile.

"I don't..." Gordon shook his head and tried to mouth the words "I don't have any cash." The man smiled and nodded, moving onto the car behind him.

HONK HONK!

Gordon looked forward and saw the light had changed back to green. He waved a *sorry* to the car behind him then drove forward.

"What now?" asked Gordon.

Charlotte's head was resting against the window. "We go on." She turned her head to look at her little brother. "We live our lives as best we can, and we make an effort to be better people than our parents were."

About the Author

Bermuda Triangle born and southern raised, T. A. Guillory lives in his hometown of New Orleans. When not writing, he spends his time gaming, going to fan conventions, and geeking out. T.A. Guillory is also the author of *The Unofficial Witcher Cookbook: Daringly Delicious Recipes for Fans of the Fantasy Classic.*

www.ingramcontent.com/pod-product-compliance
Lightning Source LLC
Chambersburg PA
CBHW031544310726
48971CB00008B/2615